PROTECT
FOREVER

—PEAK VALLEY FOREVER SERIES—

Amanda Lee Dixon

Contents

Prologue

"Let me in!" a husky voice growls outside my door.

Squinting through the peep hole, a man unfamiliar to me leers back, his murky brown eyes glaring right at me as if he can see me through the door. A cold sweat trickles down my spine, but I don't back away. I watch him semi paralyzed with fear, noting every detail from his worn tank top that stretches across a broad chest, to the words Port Pirates MC tattooed in crude lettering along the neckline. More greenish black tattoos wrap around his arms. A gun is tucked into his pants.

The gun alone should drive me to action, send me running for my phone to call for help but instead I stay rooted where I am staring into the eyes of a killer.

His monstrous fists pound harder on the door. It shudders with every blow. The metal hinges and deadbolt are no match for him, and one shot from his gun will shred my deadbolt to pieces. Splintering sounds stop my heart. He's so close to beating down my door. Faltering back a step, only partially breaking free from my panic, a dizziness clouds my vision while my lungs refuse to breathe. I have been so careful. More than careful, I have practically deleted my entire life.

"You aren't getting out alive," he whispers through the door.

I bite back a yelp, staggering back another step from the door. The door hinges are no longer flush with the frame, they are on the verge of being ripped off. Still, I stand frozen in fear. What do you do when Death stares right at you? This cannot be the end. I'm not ready for it to be the end. I dared to believe I could get away, but maybe fate has other plans.

"I'll get inside! I'll smash this fucking door down!" The menace in his voice growing with impatience.

Thunderous cracks rip through my apartment, rattling everything in its place. *Move Dawn! Now!* Tip toeing away, I shudder with every slam of his fist, trying desperately to push away my fear. If I want to get out of here alive and in one piece, I need to think.

I won't get help from my neighbors. I live on the shadier side of town where no one snitches or comes to your aide. They probably think I owe the guy money. My tiny apartment only has one way out; through the very door Death is knocking on. Snatching my phone, I wait until I'm halfway down the hallway towards my bedroom before I dial the only person who can help, Sarah.

Everything goes silent. He has stopped his pounding as if he is listening to the ringing of my phone. *Pick up!* I beg while my heart beats violently within my chest. With every ring, a choking sob escapes my throat. My door looks exhausted as it sits off center in its frame. One good kick will send it flying and spell my end.

"Dawn. Now is not a good time," Sarah sighs into the phone. Even her impatient tone is relief to my ears.

Right then, my door explodes. Splinters of wood fly across the room. Out of instinct, I duck, unable to hold back a scream. A gaping hole appears in the middle of the door, the door itself giving out before its hinges. A meaty hand reaches through the ragged opening and tugs and rips at the door, taking it apart in splintered chunks. I am almost out of time with no real plan.

"Someone's breaking in!" I cry into my phone.

Please don't let this be the end, I plead silently. Tears blur my vision. Still crouched down, I freeze. Once again fear has taken control of my body. It doesn't drive me to action. Instead it paralyzes me, rendering me defenseless.

"Hide now! I'm on my way," Sarah's voice pulls me from my blind panic. Her tone is calm.

The phone trembles in my hand, and I nod my head as if she can see me. I do my best to pull myself together. It's hard, but I'm not ready to give up.

The man's arm is sticking through the hole in the door, his hand is feeling along the frame, close to finding the deadbolt as I bolt to my bedroom.

I lock my bedroom door. It isn't enough. Grabbing my dresser, I shove with a strength I have never possessed before, and it topples over. Drawers fly open. My clothes spill at my feet. It will buy me some time. All the hiding places available in the small room are obvious: in my closet or under my bed. My bathroom is on the other side of my bed. Maybe I can fold myself to fit underneath the tiny sink cabinet.

Hearing a slam—probably my front door—vibrate my apartment, I rush around my bed towards my bathroom. I realize too late that my sink cabinet is too small. Now I am really trapped with nowhere to hide.

Window! my foggy, panic-frozen brain commands. Clambering onto the toilet, I slide open the window. I whimper when I stare down the two-story drop. Darkness swallows the pavement below. I'm staring into a bottomless pit.

Clicking noises as a hand twists my locked bedroom doorknob remind me I haven't any choices here. *Can I survive a fall from this height?* My choice made, if you could even call it a choice, I punch out the screen and maneuver one leg up while gripping the top of the window frame. With shaking hands, I somehow pull myself up. It's a tight squeeze, but I am able to turn and slide my other leg through. My legs dangle out the window. The windowsill digs into the back of my thighs. My head inside the window, I can no longer see the descent I am about to make. Twisting to see, I look down, and I see only my grave. Sucking in a deep breath—my fear brought to a whole new level—I brace myself for the fall and begin to slide my shoulders and head through the window.

An explosion of sounds bursts forth from my bedroom. A crash that can only be my dresser sends shock waves throughout the apartment. Curses, clothes and broken wood fly across the room.

I hear siren sounds in the distance. Sliding back onto the windowsill, relief floods through my system. I can't help but hiccup a nervous laugh. Help is coming.

"You fucking bitch!" The man screams as a broken drawer is hurled into the bathroom, smashing against my mirror and shattering it. I nearly lose my grip and glass shards spray over me.

Whomever he is, Death, he is livid. His breath heaves in and out from the exertion I put him through. He stares at me in the window from across the room. Seconds tick by. I wonder if he thought this was going to be an easy job.

The sirens grow louder, but I don't dare take my eyes off the man. *What is he waiting for?*

Then he decides, pulling the gun from his belt.

I don't think or hesitate. I jump.

1

- Clint -

You know what I hate more than green beans, rap music and the Raiders? Crowds. And tonight, Benny's Bar is crowded. Half the town of Peak Valley has packed themselves in for Benny's Wednesday special: domestic $10 pitchers. More of the town will file in as the night wears on, if not for the cheap beer than for Benny's legendary cheeseburger. You won't find one better. It's the best in the county.

It's not as if the people of Peak Valley have many options. We are a small town with only two bars. Benny's is on the edge of town, the outskirts really. We call it the industrial side, but others call it the wrong side of the tracks. You'll find old lumber warehouses, farming equipment dealers, and my auto body shop with its own salvage yard out back. The best part about my shop is it's across the street from Benny's.

The other side of Peak Valley is where all the small-town charm resides. Boutiques and cafes are smashed side by side with old-fashioned streetlights, decorative benches and flower beds overflowing with color. Almost every weekend there is an event that has Main Street closed. Luckily, Peak Valley doesn't experience traffic, so no one seems to mind, including me, the town recluse. I am not a recluse by nature. I like hanging at Benny's. I just prefer to be left alone. I grew up in Peak Valley. Most the people here have known me all my life, yet they cannot seem to get over how much I look like my father. He was a giant back when he was alive. Mean as hell too, and the town seems to think he passed all his genes on to me.

All my brothers were blessed with our father's height but only I'm the spitting image of him. When you grow up in a small town like Peak Valley, one that harbors preconceived notions, it's hard getting out from under your father's shadow. So you stick with your own kind and the four of us Colson boys became inseparable. We were too young to know any better, so instead of proving the town wrong, we embraced our rebel reputation. I cannot say I was surprised when my brothers one by one, moved away, but having been surrounded by them all my life, it wasn't hard to slip into a reclusive lifestyle. Sometimes, I think I should have left too. The town doesn't see me. They see my father. Charming Peak Valley maybe but don't let the charm fool you. Most of the folks around here have long memories and are too stubborn to open their eyes.

Luke, my oldest brother, always had a way with people. He is a natural born leader, but despite his military background, he has a habitual problem with being late to everything. He claims he cannot help it, but I think he's just being a douche bag who likes to be fashionable late. When he returned home from the military, he somehow managed to charm the town and became a local hero to all; except one, Amber, the night bartender at Benny's Bar.

It's Amber who greets me tonight over the noise of the people drinking on the other side of the bar as I enter Benny's.

"Hey Clint, I haven't seen you for a while," Amber shouts.

I take a seat at the end of the bar where no one else is sitting. It's quieter, tucked into the corner cast in shadows. It's the perfect spot to people watch and be left alone.

"Your usual?"

"Make it two."

"Two?" she asks with a smile and raised eyebrows. "You finally giving the female race a chance?"

"Luke's coming." I chuckle when she rolls her eyes. It's no surprise Luke chose Benny's Bar to meet up. No matter what Amber does, she cannot seem to push him away. He deserves her cold shoulder too. Years ago, he and Amber used to date, and neither of them have gotten over it. A few months into dating Amber, some chic from Luke's past claimed he was the father of her unborn baby. She was almost 7 months along and adamant it was Luke's kid. Doing what he believed was right, he ended things with Amber. Luke had just graduated from high school, but Amber was going into her junior year. He thought he was doing her a favor, letting her off the hook. Instead, he broke Amber's heart, but he wasn't around to see it. He signed with the Marines, so he would have a means to help care for the baby. He left for basic training almost immediately. During his first tour, he learned the baby wasn't his. Even heroes can have a tarnished cape. Since his return, Amber has refused to give Luke the time of day.

"Dawn. Come meet Clint," Amber yells towards the kitchen door, behind the bar. "You remember my sister Sarah?" She points to a brunette at the opposite end of the bar.

I nod a wave towards her. She was a few years younger than me in school, in my younger brother Eric's class, I think. I doubt we have ever uttered a word to each other but when you come from a small town, everyone knows everyone even if you don't run in the same circles.

I have lived in Peak Valley my entire life, except a couple of years after high school when I went to trade school to become a mechanic. My brothers and I were just small boys, barely teenagers, when a car accident took our mother's life. One day she was in my life, and the next she wasn't. The police told us she died quickly, but it brought little comfort. I hope she knew I loved her. Dad took it the hardest, and it wasn't long before he forgot all about us boys and took up the bottle. I used to think my dad was a hero. I was proud when people would tell me that I looked just like him, but then he became the town drunk. His reputation around town changed. He turned into a mean bastard. Now when the town stares at me, the spitting image of Rusty Colson, they only see a giant bully and steer clear. It's not like I've ever done anything to anyone, but I haven't tried to change anyone's mind either.

Despite the world's harsh realities, us Colson boys survived and turned out to be semi-decent men. Well, Jax, my youngest brother has me a little concerned. He was only two years old when mom died. He grew up wild, causing trouble everywhere he went, harmless crap that didn't hurt anybody. He was a good kid and can be a good man. He just has too much bullshit and a lot of balls. I have never met a person as fearless. Now, he's on some cross-country motorcycle trip. Hopefully growing up.

Eric my other younger brother is a Private Investigator in Dallas, happy to be as far away from Peak Valley as he dares to get. He would make a great detective, but his idea of justice doesn't always align with our judicial system. He is the most selfish and arrogant son of a bitch you will ever meet, with a giant chip on his shoulder, but when you need him, he's there for you. Once you get past his thick skin, he's a giant softy at the core.

It was during Eric's senior year when our father drank himself into an early grave. For years, his health was failing, but we all hoped he would hang on until I finished trade school. After his death, Eric insisted I finish my education. So, I did. Later, Jax told me about the wrestling scholarship Eric turned down. He should have accepted the scholarship. Trade school could have waited, but Eric made his decision, and I can't change it no matter how much I wish I could.

"There you are." Amber turns her attention towards the kitchen. "I want to introduce you to someone."

A pair of beautiful blue eyes peer over at me from the kitchen doorway, sucking the very breath from my lungs. They are unlike any color of blue I have ever seen. They bewitch me, ensnaring me into their sweet trap. All too suddenly, they look away, and I want to protest, make a scene, anything to get those strange blue eyes to look my way again. Still transfixed, I watch the owner of those entrancing eyes make her way towards me.

She's tiny, maybe a little over a hundred pounds, standing a few inches over five feet tall. Her face beautiful looks on the young side, maybe in her mid-twenties.

"Clint, my cousin Dawn Baker. Dawn. This is Clint Colson. He owns the auto body shop across the street." Amber makes her introductions, gesturing to each of us. Dawn flashes a shy smile, not looking at me as I extend my hand. When she looks from my hand to my eyes, I finally get another glimpse of those bewitching blue eyes. Only this time, I see more than their uniqueness. I see their sadness and a deep loneliness. Lifting her eyebrows, she seems worried, but takes my hand with one hand while tucking a strand of platinum blonde hair behind her ear with the other. The moment her dainty little hand slides into mine, tingles tickle up my arm. It's a quick shake. She breaks it off first. Her blue eyes widen, and I wonder if she felt the tingles too. For a moment she reminds me of a cornered animal with a deer-in-the-headlight look in her eyes. The look sparks a primal instinct within me to protect her, but from what?

"Good evening ladies." My brother Luke's voice bursts the bubble Dawn's presence enticed me into. He takes a seat next to me. His attention is on the one woman who wants to pretend he doesn't exist. "Amber you're looking beautiful tonight."

"Dawn you get to serve Clint since he dragged the trash in with him," Amber says ignoring Luke before storming away.

"Luke. This is Amber's cousin, Dawn." I make the introduction, trying not to laugh at his fallen face as he watches Amber's retreating backside.

Dawn steps back. She seems anxious standing alone with us. She nods her greeting towards my brother before her eyes wash over me like warm water. I cannot remember the last time a woman made me tingle, with just one touch, if one ever did. Dawn has certainly captured my attention.

"We'll take a pitcher," I say, and like Amber she rushes away. I'm not one to chase after women, but she intrigues me. She fills our pitcher. Her back is to us, and there is tension in her shoulders. Her movements are slow and hesitant, reminding me of a wounded animal. She winces as she leans over to pull chilled glasses from the freezer. That primal instinct I felt only moments ago, wants me to jump up and help her.

"Like what you see?" Luke asks, tugging my attention away. His cocky smile isn't as prominent as usual. Amber got to him more than he cares to admit. "Don't worry I can tell you have dibs."

"Only because you're sporting a hard on for Amber," I spit out as jealousy floods my system. Luke laughs. I'd gladly knock the smug smile off his face if I wasn't so shocked with myself. Me jealous? I don't think I have ever been jealous over a woman in my life. I mean I have been jealous over another man's truck, but never over a woman, especially after one brief encounter.

Dawn materializes before us carrying our pitcher and two chilled glasses. While she pours my beer, I lean in closer. She smells like brown sugar and vanilla, reminding me of a time when my mom used to bake us cookies. My mouth waters, wanting a bigger whiff. She finishes pouring my beer and begins filling Luke's glass. Our eyes meet, just for a moment, before they turn to focus on the task of pouring, and what I see surprises me, curiosity. Most women are scared of me or put off with my roughness, but never curious.

"Thank you, Sweetness," I blurt out. *Sweetness?* She smells so delicious. Not only do her eyes have some sort of hold over me but so does her sweet scent. She's turning me into a love crazed puppy.

She peers through her lashes at me, a blush creeping up her neck. "Can I get you anything else?"

Yeah, I'm going to keep calling her Sweetness.

"We're good," I say out loud.

A smile spreads across my face, but I don't let myself lean in for another whiff of her scent, pressing my hands against the bar so hard my knuckles turn white. I play it cool. I don't want to frighten her away just yet.

"Careful or we might need a new bar," Luke chuckles after Dawn is a safe distance away. "Besides, I need your full attention, I have news."

"You're getting your face fixed?" I ask, turning towards him, releasing my hold on the bar.

"This perfect mug? Never," he dishes back, taking a big gulp from his beer. He waits a second making sure he has my attention. Luke always liked being the center of attention. "I bought the old warehouse next to your shop."

"What?" My eyebrows go up. I wait for him to tell me he's joking. The warehouse he is talking about has sat abandon since before I bought my shop. It's not in terrible shape, withstanding years of abandonment; but still, it seems like a risky investment.

"I need a place to build and what better place than next to my little brother," he exclaims messing my hair up with the palm of one hand.

"Did you buy it solely because it was next to the shop?" I ask, shoving his hand away. His confidence falters for a moment, and I wonder if having it next door was a big deciding factor.

Clenching his jaw, he looks away. The tension in his neck muscles make his veins budge. Maybe Amber didn't get to him after all and his nerves are shaking over his new purchase. "It's more space than I need but I'll be able to expand, and the price tag was cheap," he justifies more to himself than to me. "I had it inspected and there's nothing terribly wrong with it. Stuff I can take care of."

"You sure about this?" I ask, studying him closely. "You want to build tiny homes for the rest of your life?"

"There's a market for them, and I can do all the work myself without a crew to worry about." Luke recites while rubbing the back of his neck. "Plus, tiny homes won't tie up all my money if the market slows."

"I guess congratulations are in order. You're the newest tiny home contractor in what… all of Kansas?" I raise my beer glass and give him my cheers.

"Nah. There are a few others but not for at least a hundred-mile radius," Luke informs me. His shoulders relax as his cocky smile breaks loose. "I'll close on the building around the same time I finish the first-floor model."

"As long as you know what you are getting yourself into you will do just fine," I affirm. "As a business owner I can attest to a lot of nights working for free, long hours, and at times you think you might fail. It's scary, but it has its pros, too. You get to make up your own hours. You can hire someone to do the shit you don't want to do, and you don't have to answer to anyone."

"Thanks Clint." Luke's cocky grin spreads from ear to ear as he squeezes my shoulder.

"How's Mom and Dad's old place coming along?" I ask.

"It's in desperate need of a little TLC, but overall the bones are good. Finishing up the floor model will keep me busy for a while, delaying work on the house," he says, topping off our glasses and stealing a glance at Amber as she walks past us. It doesn't take a genius to know what Luke is thinking but I say nothing. Luke needs to man up and take Amber by the horns and reconcile their differences. I don't know why he's holding back.

I steal a quick glance over my shoulder. Dawn looks lost in her own thoughts while she stands by Sarah who seems to be sitting alone. There is an uneasiness to Dawn in the way she hugs her body. It bothers me. Dawn catches me staring at her. Those bewitching eyes so full of sadness are like a punch to the chest, and I am powerless to do anything about it.

"Can we get another one?" I call out, my voice cracking like a damn teenage boy. Dawn turns to grab another pitcher, and I zero in on her ass. Standing before me is a fragile woman, and I'm checking her out without shame.

"You have it bad," Luke mutters into his beer with a smug smile before draining the glass.

Helping himself, he fills his glass. Our pitcher is still a quarter full.

"Shut up," I growl at his silent laughter. I drain my beer and fill my glass. Dawn reaches us, setting the full pitcher down and collecting our now empty one.

"You two want any food?" She asks, peeking up at me, our eyes connecting like magnets.

"Depends. Is Benny cooking?" Luke breaks in capturing Dawn's attention, making me want to punch him.

"He isn't working today."

Amber sweeps past Dawn carrying two more pitchers doing her best to ignore Luke, but I saw her glance at him. He watches her make her way toward a rowdy group of men close to the bar playing pool. Dawn also watches her, nervously biting her lips.

"Are they causing trouble?" I ask. Her eyes seek mine with a puzzled expression.

"No…." Her answer trails off. The color drains from her face. Following her line of sight over my shoulder, Luke is already off his chair making a beeline for the pool tables. It takes me a second to see what's going on before I recognize Amber sandwiched between two jackasses trying to get her to dance. Tim McGraw's, "I Like It, I Love It" is blaring over the juke box, and these clueless pricks are doing a piss-poor job singing it while rubbing up against her.

Fuck this won't end well.

Luke makes it to Amber in record time. Grabbing her forearm, he pulls her free. Lurching away from the jackasses, she almost drops the empty glasses she's holding, but Luke steadies her, pulling her close. I know that dangerous glint in his eye. It means trouble if I don't defuse the situation, and quick.

"What the hell?" one dumbass cries out looking down at his beer-soaked shirt. A couple of guys move in on Luke, and I'm out of my seat to help him.

People automatically move out of my way, watching, waiting for something to happen.

"Let's settle down." I say stepping between Luke and the pissed off men. Several pairs of eyes turn to glare up at me, hesitating as they take in my large frame. Even outnumbered, these guys are no match for Luke and me. But I don't want to get in a fight. These jackasses are sporting big dick attitudes feeling invincible from too much to drink. It wouldn't be a fair fight.

I send Amber a don't-question-me look and command, "Get Luke back to his seat."

She doesn't protest.

Luke's jaw muscles clench and unclench. He looks ready to say something, but Amber lays a hand on his chest, and whatever was brewing in his thoughts clears.

"Come on," she says as she tugs on his arm. Reluctantly he follows her back to our seats.

"No harm was done. Let's let bygones be bygones," I suggest to the group. I look every single one in the eye. They all take a step closer still holding their pool sticks.

"And if we don't?" One of them challenges turning his face up at me like he isn't scared.

Looking down at the man, he is at least a foot shorter than I am and carries most of his weight in his gut. I can smell the stench of beer on his breath. Sweat beads from his brow. These guys aren't fighters. They, like most men are only confrontational when surrounded by their buddies and their bellies full of liquid courage.

It isn't hard for me to get under their skin, spook them a but with a scowl, while sizing each one up. Doubt sets in and that's when you let them walk away. Most men are smart enough to take the opportunity to tuck tail and run.

"I don't think you guys want any trouble."

"I don't know," the short man says and rubs his jaw with a smirk. "Trouble sounds like fun." Obviously this one isn't that smart.

"C-mon, Vern. Let's finish our game," one of his friends suggests. Smart man.

"What about my buddy's beer? Your friend made him spill it," the man called Vern says. He smiles while eyeing me. Nope, not the sharpest tool in the shed. He's a glutton for punishment.

My patience is unprecedented, but I can't say I wouldn't mind knocking him upside the head.

"Vern drop it. You shouldn't have messed with Benny's daughter." Another one of his friends' pipes in.

The other two, who haven't spoken, mutter something to each other before leaving Vern for their unfinished pool game.

"A bunch of pussies!" Vern shouts as the rest of his buddies abandon him.

I continue to stare down at him before he shrugs and walks away. Maybe he does have some sense after all. Not a lot, but some.

Heading back, I spot Dawn's platinum blonde hair like a beacon of bright light. She is watching me with open curiosity. Sarah is also watching, shifting narrowed eyes from me to Dawn. Amber whispers into Luke's ear. His hand stays on her hip as he watches me approach.

"Thank you," Amber says when I sit down next to a more relaxed Luke.

"Yeah. Thanks," Luke mutters patting my back with his free hand, still holding Amber's hip with the other.

"You boys want a burger?" Amber asks quickly stepping away from Luke's hand. I see her sudden move to put distance between them is not lost on Luke.

"Sure," I say looking away from the two of them. I don't want to see Luke's disappointment especially after coming to Amber's aide.

"Coming right up," she says with a forced smile. Turning, she disappears into the kitchen, clearly not happy she let her guard down around Luke.

"You're welcome," Luke murmurs, leaning close, his cocky grin sliding across his face.

"For what?"

"For making you look good in front of the new bartender," He smirks.

Such an arrogant dick! I think. Only he can change his mood like a light switch.

"Shut up, you jerk. You're lucky I was here to clean your shit up," I mutter quietly, sensing Dawn approaching us.

"Need anything?" she asks, tucking a stray hair behind her ear.

I want to be the one to tuck her hair behind her ear.

"We're good, Sweetness," I say not stopping myself from leaning forward to take in her delicious scent while whispering, "Maybe next time I can get a smile out of you."

The briefest of smiles appears. I grin back at her and watch a blush flush her porcelain skin before she rushes back to the other end of the bar.

I have never had much charm, it always seemed like a waste of time. If I liked a girl, I let her know it, but there is something vulnerable about Dawn. I doubt my bluntness and boorish manners will win her over.

So, what the hell am I going to do?

2

- Dawn -

You know what I hate more than green beans, humidity, and spiders? Crowds. They put me on edge and my already frayed nerves are close to plunging me into a straight panic. Why did I agree to this? Bartending only weeks after fleeing town, and I am still looking over my shoulder praying no one followed.

"Relax," Sarah hisses from the other side of the bar. Her emerald green eyes study me closely looking for signs of panic before reminding me, "You're safe."

I'm not so sure that's true, I think, but I don't say it. I just nod my head and try to mask the fear I'm sure is plastered on my face. Sarah's plan sounded perfect when she proposed the idea while I was recovering in the hospital: Move to Kansas, live in her parent's old two-bedroom home and fill in at her dad's bar. Benny was having a hard time finding a replacement bartender, since Amber plans to leave soon. It was Amber's idea to make me a distant cousin.

"If you're going to work for Daddy and live in my parent's old house, you might as well call him Uncle Benny," Amber stated while showing me around my first night at the bar. Just like that I became Dawn Baker.

I don't know anyone who would believe we are remotely related. We look nothing alike. For starters, Sarah and Amber both have the same emerald green eyes and long chestnut brown hair, where I have a weird shade of blue eyes and platinum blonde hair. I am also petite, like I haven't finished growing with a baby face. Sarah and Amber are both mature looking with tall elegant figures. Not to mention in this town everyone knows everyone and their history. Benny and his wife Linda are respected around Peak Valley, so if they tell the town I'm a distant relative no one's going to question. If I'm lucky I might just melt into the background and no one will ever find me again.

"What are you thinking about over there?" Sarah asks pulling me from my thoughts and reminding me I'm surrounded by strangers in a crowded bar. For a moment I forgot all about my nerves and dared to hope Sarah's plan could work.

"Nothing," I smile, wishing I had the words to tell her how grateful I am for everything she has done. I owe her a life-time worth of gratitude. "Why are you looking at me like that? What do you want?"

"Nothing. *Sweetness.* I'm good," Sarah chuckles into her beer. "You should go check on your new admirer."

"I was dreading your departure. Now, not so much." I roll my eyes and hope she doesn't notice the short glance I throw towards Clint. The man isn't hard to miss. He is built like an ox with a scowl and icy blue eyes that should terrify me but don't.

"Liar." Sarah's smile spreads wider.

"I think you've had enough," I say taking her half empty beer and tossing it into the trash bin. Sarah laughs as I do my best to ignore her while helping a customer. Out of the corner of my eye, I see that Clint watches me. He has watched me all night, his face unrevealing, his black hair surrounds handsome features that are intimidating in a scary, yet sexy kind of way. People seem to be uncomfortable around him, except his brother Luke, whom I notice is only uncomfortable around Amber.

I wish I knew what he was thinking... *What? No!* I don't want to know what Clint's thinking! I shouldn't even be thinking about Clint. I should be thinking about... nothing, because there is nothing for me to think about other than keeping my head down and blending in.

"Sweetness." Amber purrs from close behind me.

"Frick!" I cry out, faltering back a step. It doesn't take much to scare me these days. The doctors said it would likely happen after the jump, but even the most minor encounters can trigger a scare in me.

"Sorry hon." Amber frowns, her hands carrying two plates stacked high with fries and Benny's famous cheeseburgers. "Grab me some utensils please."

Shaking my head, I don't trust my voice, not that I could hear it over the roaring in my ears. Reaching for the rolled-up utensils, my hand visibly shakes while my heart rate shows no signs of slowing. I take a shaky breath; it does nothing to calm me. Neither does a deep breath.

Clint is still watching me. For a moment concern flashes across his face, calming me enough to follow Amber who's already placed Clint's plate before him. Setting Luke's plate down, she doesn't slide it towards him but begins putting the fixings on his cheeseburger. First, she adds a little ketchup, then a sliver of mayo. She tops it with lettuce and tomato before flipping it over and adding more ketchup. I watch her work, holding back a snicker. When she's done, she slides the plate to Luke, her smile bright and for once she doesn't look upset with him.

"Just the way I like it." He smiles down at his food before catching Amber's eye. The air begins to sizzle around the two as unspoken words float between them. Amber snaps out of it first. Her smile quickly turns into a frown while Luke's fades altogether.

Interesting. I'll have to get Sarah to tell me what happened between the two of them.

"Don't get used to it," Amber huffs, walking away leaving me alone with the Colson men.

"Ouch," Clint mutters before biting into his cheeseburger. It looks like a child-sized portion in his hands.

"And, she's back to being pissed at me." Luke sighs, grabbing a handful of fries and stuffing them into his mouth.

"Mind handing me those?" Clint asks, nodding his head towards the rolled utensils I am still holding.

My cheeks flush with embarrassment, and I quickly place them in front of him. Turning away, I rush to the other end of the bar.

"You have to admit Clint is a steamy piece of meat." Sarah winks with a knowing smile when I reach her.

Shaking my head, my cheeks still burning, I don't want to admit how true her words are. Even in a simple grey shirt and faded old jeans, Clint looks like he could be a male model—albeit a scary looking male model, but gorgeous all the same. "Colson's Auto Body Shop and Repair" stretches across his wide chest. His arm muscles are like sculpted marble, and his hands have seen years of hard work.

"The last thing I need is a man. No matter how steamy he is," I say more to myself than to Sarah. My recent near-death experience should serve as a reminder. Haven't I learned? Men equal trouble.

"No one said you couldn't have any fun," Sarah teases. A mischievous smile curves across her face.

A small spark of excitement shoots through me and makes it hard not to smile back. "With my luck, I'll have to move again and be someone else's fake cousin," I smirk rolling my eyes playfully. I don't dare admit to her how much I like being her and Amber's fake distant cousin. Admitting it will jinx it, and I am *not* ready to let go of what Sarah has created for me. If I am not careful, I might even grow attached to my fake family, making it hard to leave when I am found again.

"No one said it has to be serious. Letting loose would do your body good," Sarah says with an encouraging smile. It isn't the first time she's tried to coax me out of my self-appointed exile, since arriving in Peak Valley.

Isn't working at Benny's Bar enough?

"I need to head out. Mom wants to have dinner." Sarah stands stretching after sitting for several hours keeping me company. I am a selfish friend, keeping her away from her parents, her job, and her life, and for what? So, I can have peace of mind while I work at her dad's bar.

Someday I will pay her back. I hope. "I can't believe you're leaving tomorrow."

Sarah pauses putting her coat on.

I didn't mean to sound so disheartened. She and I have talked about her returning to Charleston, but it doesn't change the fact that after tomorrow I'll lose the one person who makes me feel safe.

"You're safe here," Sarah says as if reading my mind. She zips up her coat and pulls her hair from the collar as the phone behind the bar rings.

"I'll see you after dinner." She waves as she turns from the bar.

I feel a lonely pang in my chest as I nod and attempt to smile. "Benny's Bar," I answer the phone, watching Sarah maneuver through the crowd and out the front door, disappearing into the brisk fall night.

"Amber?" A female voice on the other end asks.

"No. This is Dawn. Can I help you?"

"I'm looking for Mr. Burns," the woman replies. She sounds impatient. "Can you tell me if he is there."

"It's pretty crowded." I relay back to her. Benny's Bar isn't big but pack it in with people and it's near impossible to see everyone. "What does he look like?"

"Like an annoying old man who should be in his bed!" The woman grumbles from the other end. "I'm Cindy, his nurse, at the assisted living home he has currently escaped from."

"And you think he's here?" I frown still looking around. Several patrons are older in age, but none look like they belong in a nursing home.

"Who are you looking for Sweetness?" Clint's gruff voice calls out from the opposite side of the bar. I can feel his eyes wash over me from head to toe. Every time he uses the pet name a blush burns my cheeks.

"Mr. Burns," I say rather loudly unable to look him in the eye. The way he watches me makes my stomach warm and my chest heavy.

"Old Man Burns sneak out again?" Luke cuts in with an amused smirk. "Tell Cindy he hasn't made it here yet but give him time. He's old."

"Who are you calling, *old*?" A man with thinning white-hair plops down next to Clint. He looks to be in his late seventies, and I have no doubt that's the man Cindy is looking for. "When I ran the auto shop," the old man complained, "I didn't have time to fraternize like you yuppies."

"Yuppies?" Clint rolls his eyes. His smile widens.

"I think your Mr. Burns just got here," I tell Cindy.

Next to Clint, the old man looks frail and small, and I wonder how he even made it through the crowd of people to the bar. One strong wind would knock him over.

"Who's the new chick and why is she eyeing me like I'm about to keel over?" the old man asks as all three of them look up at me.

"Tell Cindy I'll get him home safe, but I doubt sound. He's elderly." Luke winks at me.

"Luke says he will get him home," I repeat into the phone, hoping they can't see my blush. "Luke Colson," I add.

"Wonderful. Thank you," Cindy answers, relieved.

"You're welcome." I hang up the phone.

"As I live and breathe, Burns. How did you escape Cindy's watchful eye?" Amber hails from the kitchen doorway, walking around the bar. Only glancing at Luke for a moment, she wraps her arms around Burns and kisses his cheek.

"I heard you were leaving soon and thought I'd come pay you a visit," Burns says into her hair.

"You're leaving?" Luke asks in disbelief. "Where?"

Glancing at Luke, she softens for a moment before turning her attention back to Burns. "I accepted a position at the hospital. I'll be working nights. More pay and more hours," she tells him. "Might even see you there if you keep sneaking out."

"I'm fit as a fiddle! Uptight Cindy needs to get a life." Burns waves her away.

"When do you start?" Luke asks grabbing Amber's upper arm as she passes him.

Looking down at where Luke's hand holds her before straightening her shoulders and fixing him with a look that would put anyone to shame, she hisses, "It is none of your business, Luke Colson. Now let me go."

"Oh, let the poor man know," Burns shrugs.

"In a week," she mumbles, sulking around the bar to my side.

"And who might you be?" Burns asks fixing two watery eyes on me.

"Dawn. New bartender," I answer matter-of-factly. It sounded rehearsed even to me, but it is all true. My name is Dawn. I am the new bartender. So why do I feel like such a phony?

"Dawn's my cousin. Moved all the way from South Carolina to be closer to family," Amber steps in to say. She makes the lie sound real, topping it off with a genuine smile. She nearly has me fooled into believing I am really part of the Baker family. "Daddy needed a new bartender, and Dawn was so gracious to help."

"Cousin you say?" Burns narrows his eyes at me. "Who do you belong to?"

"Belong to?" I ask, trying to swallow the sudden lump that wants to clog my throat.

"She's a distant cousin. You wouldn't have met her parents," Amber chimes in, her smile growing serious, saving the day yet again. "But forget all that, what can we get you Burns?"

"Tall PBR."

"Coming right up." She hooks my arm with hers dragging me to the other end of the bar. "That was close."

"Too close." I whisper, looking over my shoulder. Both Burns and Clint watch us, "I don't think they bought it."

"Sure, they did." She releases my arm, opening the beer cooler she pulls out a PBR and a chilled glass. "What's not to believe."

"It feels wrong lying to everyone." I confess. A damn lump in my throat doing its best to gag me. "The truth usually finds a way out."

"Sweetness," she faces me with a tender smile, "It isn't a lie. The details might be made up, but you *are* family."

So many emotions hit me hard in the chest all at once. Her words made an impact that brought tears burning the back of my throat.

"Oh, don't cry."

"I won't," I choke out desperate to hold in a sob. "It's hard not to. You all have been so nice to me."

"Go take a break and wash your face. I can handle the bar," she suggests, tossing the empty PBR can in the trash on her way to deliver Burns' beer.

Rushing through the kitchen, I head for the back door that leads to a small "Employees Only" area. Chilly autumn air hits my face, and the tears I held back fall freely down my cheeks. It has been too long since I was part of a family.

Ten years ago, I lost my mother in a car accident. She had so much joy for life to have died so young. She was so beautiful too. Every day she made me feel loved. I cherish every memory I have of her.

I remember the day she died as if it was yesterday. I was only fourteen years old. I was waiting for her to come home from work. It was late and my mother was never late getting home. I was beginning to worry when someone knocked on our apartment door. I almost didn't open the door when I saw two police officers and an older woman on the other side.

"Do you mind if we come in?" the woman asked when I finally did open the door. Her smile was sympathetic. It makes me angry just thinking about it.

"My mother isn't home," I tell her. Somewhere in the back of my mind, I knew why they were there.

"We want to talk to you about your mother," the woman says, and she takes a step closer to the door. I want to slam it in her face. "It's better if we talk inside."

I let them in, the officers stay standing while the woman introduces herself and takes a seat next to me on the couch. I cannot remember her name, nor the police officers. I can still picture their faces, but I cannot remember their names.

"Dawn, we have some unfortunate news," she says taking my hand. I want to pull away from her but that would be rude, and my mother always told me to respect my elders, so I let her cold hands wrap around mine. "Do you have any family we can call?"

"Family?" I squeak. My throat wanted to close up and not answer any of her questions.

"Your father? Maybe an Aunt?" she asks.

"I don't know my father, and my mother doesn't have any family." I get the words out, my breath catching on every one. The woman pats my hand and nods.

"Dawn. I am really sorry. I have to tell you this, but your mother was killed in an accident…"

I don't remember what else she said. My tears rolled down my face, and all I wanted to do in that moment was scream, but I didn't. My whole world was torn from me, and I just silently cried while the woman helped me pack up some of my belongings.

I went into foster care that night, and like so many teenagers who enter the system, I drifted from family to family.

Not a single family I stayed with welcomed me in—made me one of their own—not like the Bakers have. I finally have the opportunity to be a part of a family, yet a piece of my heart won't let me believe it because, deep down, I know the Port Pirates Motorcycle Club is still out there. They won't stop looking for me, not until they find me.

3

- Clint -

I hate grocery shopping. I find it tedious and boring but watching the beauty comb through apples in skinny jeans that accentuate her ass has made it my new favorite chore.

"Need any help, Sweetness?" I ask her from behind. She is so lost in her inspection of the apples she never heard me come up.

"Frick!" she cries out, dropping the apples to the ground, tripping and falling backwards into my chest. Steading her, my hands itch to pull her closer into my chest and wrap her up in my arms. Instead, I let her take a couple of shaky breathes and release her. I pick up the fallen apples as she watches me with those bewitching blue eyes that are glazed over in fear.

"I...sorry," she whispers. With shaking hands, she tries to reach for the apples I am holding, but I stop her.

"No. I'm sorry. I shouldn't have snuck up on you."

I put the apples back into the bin. Silence falls between us. Dawn has the look of a wounded animal. She watches me like I cornered her into a trap. I know the look of fear this town has for me, and I never bothered to change their opinions, but seeing Dawn's terrified look fills me with shame.

The shame alone should send me on my way, but it is nothing compared to the primal need to stay by Dawn's side until she's calmed down; and even then, I am not sure I'll want to leave her. I cannot explain what is going on in my chest. It is foreign and uncomfortable, yet I don't want it to go away.

"I should go." Dawn finally speaks. Her voice no longer sounds strangled with fear. "I have a lot of shopping to get done."

"Mind if I join you?" I ask, taking a step back so she can get to her shopping cart. I didn't realize how close we were. The scent of brown sugar and vanilla fades a little, and I regret allowing the slightest distance between us.

"Um... I guess." She nervously bites her lip. "You don't have to."

"I want to," I tell her as we start maneuvering through the produce section. "I hate shopping, so you'll be doing me a favor keeping me company."

"What if I'm not good company?" she asks, stopping by a bin of green leafy stuff I wouldn't dare eat unless forced.

"I doubt it." I smirk. Her bewitching blues catch mine, and a blush starts to color her cheeks. My smile grows. She's cute when she blushes. I never thought of myself as a man who likes cute, but Dawn seems to be changing a lot of things about me. Most of the women I have been with were loud, demanding and selfish. They would use me like I would use them. It was mutually beneficial. But, I have no desire to use Dawn. The thought of anyone using Dawn pisses me off.

"I love food shopping," she admits. She tears her eyes from mine and turns her back. Watching her inspect the produce is fascinating and weirdly attractive. I must be going soft if a woman can make sniffing vegetables look sexy.

"What is that?" I ask when she throws a bundle that looks like lettuce into her cart.

"Kale," she answers, leading us back towards the apples again. "It's good source of protein. I like it in salads or smoothies."

"Rabbit food," I mutter, grabbing a bunch of bananas. *I should eat better*, I tell myself, putting them into the cart. I am not trying to impress Dawn. *I like bananas*, I justify to myself.

"What is on your shopping list?" Dawn asks with a smile while focusing on plucking apples from the bin. The way she is bent over in those skinny jeans reminds me that I am a hot-blooded male whose pants are starting to get a little too tight.

"I don't really have a list." I quickly adjust the growing bulge while her attention is elsewhere. "I just grab whatever looks good."

"And what exactly looks good today?"

You! I want to say but stop myself. Dawn looks ripe and juicy, but she's shy with a touch of innocence I am not use too. I have to navigate more cautiously with her.

"All you have is meat and chips."

"Man food," I say.

"Man food," she repeats. Her smile grows bigger before she shakes her head and laughs softly.

I am not prepared for the stoppage of my heart. She's even more beautiful when she looks happy, all trace of fear gone. I am not a funny man, but I'll become a comedian if it will make her smile and laugh like this.

"You'll give yourself a heart attack with all that red meat."

"Eh." I shrug. "I'm not much of a cook, but I can grill."

"I like to cook," she admits with a ghost of a smile, leading us out of the produce section and down the baking aisle. "But I love to bake."

"What's your favorite thing to bake?" I ask. I want to know everything about her, and right now she isn't being shy.

"It depends on the mood I'm in." She scans the contents on the shelves, grabbing items as we go. "I love baking cookies when I'm happy, pound cake when I'm sad, and pastries when I'm feeling adventurous." Dawn continues to talk about baking as we walk from aisle to aisle filling her cart with food. I listen to her talk about the best brands and how the secret to a moist pound cake is to use sour cream. Filing these tidbits of information away, I prompt her to talk more about baking or cooking. It's my ticket to getting her to let her guard down.

I have finished my shopping some time ago, but don't say anything, following Dawn as she loops us back to the baking aisle.

"I think I'm going to make Linda and Benny some cookies," she says, and my heart skips a beat knowing that baking cookies means she's happy, and I can't help but think that I am the reason for her happiness.

"What for?"

"For everything they've done." She shrugs stopping before the chocolate chips. "They didn't have to help me, but they did. I have never met a nicer family."

"Aren't they *your* family?" I question. She is talking as if they aren't her family, or maybe she doesn't feel a part of their family?

"Yes—they are—they are my, my family," she stammers, her shoulders tensing. "I just meant they didn't have to help, but they did."

"That is what family does. They help each other," I comment watching her closely. There is something off about her story.

"Right." She snatches several bags of chocolate chips and tosses them into her cart.

"I'm ready to check out," she says. She leads us towards the registers, her steps quickening.

"Me too." I follow her.

Dawn's cart is fuller than mine, so I move to the lane next to her. When I'm finished, she is nearly done checking out, so I wait.

"You don't have to wait for me," she says, pulling a wad of cash from her wallet.

"I wouldn't be much of a gentleman if I didn't offer to help load your groceries into your car."

The cashier watches us with wide eyes and concern. I know her from high school but can't remember her name. Glancing at her name tag, I see it reads, 'Betty.' That's right, Betty was in the class ahead of me, Luke's class. I should say hi, maybe smile, but she looks ready to call the cops on me, and I rather focus on Dawn and her sudden agitation with me.

"I can manage." Dawn hands over the cash with a smile that does little to comfort the cashier, before shifting her gaze my way.

"I have no doubt you can," I flash her a smile, "but my mom would turn over in her grave if I didn't help."

"Your mom… she passed away?" Dawn asks with sympathy in her eyes as she collects her change and puts it in her wallet.

"She passed when I was a kid." I share as we push our carts towards the exit.

"I'm sorry." Dawn lays her hand on my forearm. The tingles I felt when we first met race up my arm. "My mother passed away when I was fourteen. I know how painful it must have been."

"I'm sorry you lost your mom." I lay a hand over hers. She doesn't pull away for several seconds as we share a moment of grief. I follow her out of the store. She stops in front of an older 90's Toyota that I believe belongs to Linda Baker.

"This is mine," Dawn says. Pulling the keys from her purse, she unlocks the trunk. I help her load her groceries. The chilly autumn air causes Dawn to shiver.

"Where is your coat?" I ask, shutting her trunk.

"I left it at home."

Grabbing the empty cart, I walk with her to the cart stall. "You'll need to start wearing it," I mumble, realizing our time together is almost over. "Do you work tonight?"

"No, I'm off today and tomorrow," she says, her teeth slightly chattering as the wind begins to pick up. "I better go." She hugs her body for warmth.

"Would you like to have dinner with me?" I ask, not sounding like my grumpy self. I sound hopeful, maybe even a little eager. I don't think I have ever asked a woman to dinner. Usually they do the asking, or more like, the telling.

"Dinner?" She looks down at her feet. My stomach drops when a pair of conflicted blues look up at me. "I can't tonight."

"Tomorrow?"

"I can't."

"When can you?"

I narrow my eyes at her trying to figure out what she's thinking. She's not turning me down because she isn't interested. She is definitely interested. I can tell by the expression in her eyes, the look on her face. She's rejecting me for some unknown reason and it's tearing her up inside.

"I mean. I'm not in a place where I can date," she explains with regret in her voice. "I'm sorry."

"Dawn…" I trail off when she looks away. Either the biting wind or turning me down has brought tears to her eyes.

"Sorry," she says again. Turning around, she walks away, and I know I'm fucked because even though she has turned me down, I'm not giving up.

4

- Dawn -

"Come on! Start you stupid thing!" I yell at my car, but it's no use. It just keeps clicking. Resting my forehead on the steering wheel, a single tear drops from my cheek onto my jeans. Between turning Clint down only minutes ago and now a dead car, my life truly cannot get worse. "Please start," I whisper to the car, hoping it will have mercy on me. The look on Clint's face when I turned him down about knocked me off my feet. He looked like a puppy dog that realized he was being left home alone for the first time.

"Need some help?"

"Frick!"

My head snaps back. My heart pounds against my rib cage, and for the second time today, Clint has nearly managed to give me a heart attack. He is like a giant ninja the way he sneaks up on me. I am not sure my heart can take much more.

Opening the driver's door, I step out of the car into the brisk autumn air. My hands tremble, and I am grateful the wind nips at my cheeks because it masks my tears. I keep the open car door between Clint and me. I can't look into his eyes.

"My car won't start."

"I noticed," Clint replies, stepping around the door. He stops when I start to retreat back into my car.

"Can I have a look?" he asks.

"Oh. Yes." I stumble over my words.

Why am I such an idiot right now?

"I mean no. I don't want to trouble you."

"No trouble." Clint takes another step leaving little space between us.

"Mind letting me in?" he asks, pointing to the driver seat. "I just want to pop the hood and listen to it try to start up."

Nodding, because I have lost the ability to speak, I slide past him, unable to avoid touching him. The hardness of his body ignites mine, stopping my need to move away. The cold no longer has an effect on me, but Clint sure does. It has been so long since I have felt any sort of attraction to a man. I thought my body would forever be dormant.

"Sweetness." Clint's voice is gentle. He leans close to my ear. His breathe tickles my neck. "I need you to move out of the way." There is laughter in his voice. Carefully, he puts two hands on my shoulders and moves me backwards. My face must be beet red, but Clint doesn't notice, turning away he opens the hood and tries the engine. To my relief, his focus is now on my car.

"Your battery is dead," Clint says. He managed to fold himself into my tiny Toyota and makes it look easy to climb out of it. Parts of my face still burn with embarrassment.

"I'll pull my truck around."

"I don't have cables."

"I have some."

I watch him walk away, but he turns back.

"Put this on," he says, shrugging off his coat. Clint doesn't hand it to me. He opens it to help me put it on. "C-mon. It's too cold for you to be without a coat."

"What about you?" I ask. I hesitate to walk forward, so he closes the distance between us, wrapping it around my shoulders. The coat is three, maybe four, times too big, but warm and smells of gasoline and something earthy. The combination is comforting. Again, I watch Clint walk away, his hands tucked deep into his pockets. His back muscles and broad shoulders stretch his shirt. He walks with confidence, as if I haven't just rejected him. Taking a deep breath, inhaling Clint's scent, I force myself to look away.

Every fiber in my being told me to accept Clint's offer to have dinner. I can even hear the imaginary Sarah in my head yelling at me for being a coward, but it's for the best not to get involved with anyone. I don't want to jump the gun. I just moved here. Who knows how long I get to stay. It wouldn't be fair to either of us.

I try not to watch Clint work, but I am too weak. Every time he looks at me, my stomach does a somersault. His eyes are gentle and scary all at once. It's impossible to think. I don't dare go near the car. I don't trust myself. He must think I am rude.

"Should be charged enough to get you home." Clint shuts my hood, pulling a rag from his back pocket to wipe his hands. "If you bring her by my shop, I can see if your battery needs to be replaced."

"I should talk to Benny first," I say, and he nods his head. Still wiping his hands, he studies me like he did at Benny's Bar the other night. It's kind of scary and intimidating. I wonder what he is thinking.

"Thank you," I say.

"No worries."

"Do I owe you something?"

If I thought he was scary before, I saw a glimpse of something nightmares are made of flash across his face.

"Like dinner?" he asks, raising an eyebrow. He looks angry.

"Yeah," I reply just above a whisper.

"I don't know what kind of guy you think I am, but I won't twist your arm to have dinner with me."

My stomach drops at his words.

"That's not what I meant."

"But you thought it," he retorts, tucking the rag back into his pocket, and with one long stride he is standing right in front of me. I have to tilt my head back to see his strong jaw as it clenches. My heart begins to pound, and I'm at a loss for words. I never was good with them.

"You aren't the first to think the worst and, you won't be the last."

"I didn't think that," I whisper. "I was just... trying to be polite."

"Polite?" His eyes soften as his mouth cracks in a smile that could be mistaken for devilish.

"Yes. Polite," I repeat, unable to stop the shy smile from spreading across my own mouth. The air around us crackles with an energy only Clint and I can feel.

"Well then, how about a batch of your homemade cookies?" He smirks down at me.

"Ok." My smile grows.

"You better go." He nods towards my car. "It's cold."

Reluctantly, I step around him and get into my car before I look at him again. Waving, I shut the door and fasten my seat belt while he watches with his intense, scary eyes. Yet, I can find tenderness in them.

I back out of the parking place and drive away while he watches me. Sucking in a deep breath, I realize I never gave him his coat back; so, I take another deep breath and let his scent calm me.

5

- Clint -

Avoiding Benny's should have been easy. I don't frequent it much, but Dawn won't leave my thoughts and paying a visit just to see her is enticing. I know nothing about her, yet she plays through my mind as if my entire world should revolve around her. I tried making her just another pretty face but have not been successful. Her bewitching blue eyes prey on me. Those eyes are a shade of blue that I have never seen before, swirling with a sadness that haunts me. That alone should be enough to warn me away, but clearly my head and my gut are not on the same page.

My phone buzzes in my pocket. I pull it out and groan when I see Cindy's number on the display. "How can I help you, Cindy?" I ask.

"Sorry to bother you Clint, but I can't find Mr. Burns again," she sighs into the phone. "I have called around, but no one has seen him.

Poor thing has her hands full with Burns.

"Have you checked Benny's?" I ask, trying not to chuckle. I know she hates it when I don't take Burns' roaming seriously, but he's been running off for years. If it was any other resident, they'd have kicked him out, but after the assisted living facility lost their maintenance man, Burns started picking up the responsibilities for them. It started off as something to keep him busy, but now it is a mutually beneficial situation, much to Cindy's dismay. If she had her way, she would lock Burns up. However, the facility saves money; and in return, they turn a blind eye to his wandering. Not that he's in any danger; the man will out-live us all.

"The new girl at Benny's sounded unsure. I think she's covering for him." Cindy's tone drips with disapproval. "Do you mind checking Benny's for me?"

"You sure that he isn't at the Rec Center? It's lady's bingo night," I ask, knowing I can't get out of going to Benny's.

"I'm heading to the Rec Center now, actually," Cindy says. "Mr. Burns has been a little dizzy these past couple of days. More than anything, I'm more worried he will take a fall."

I sigh a little too loudly.

"Please do me this favor," she begs.

"I'm on it." I am already heading out the door as I say it. Remembering how badly Burns' hands were shaking the other night puts speed in my step, building my uneasiness over his health.

Burns is the closest thing I have to a father. He was there for my brothers and I when we needed someone in our corner. He helped pick up the pieces when Luke lost Amber; he stepped in when my little brother Jax needed a firm hand; he gave me a job and eventually gave me his treasure when he sold the auto body shop to me. Confronting Burns with his declining health makes

me feel like I am over-stepping a boundary—
violating the trust of the man who has done so
much for my brothers and me.

I feel a lump in my throat and hesitate before
I ask, "Is he ok?"

She hesitates too and starts slowly, "He's
healthy for an 86-year-old but he needs to be more
careful. He isn't as young as he used to be."

I let out the breath I didn't realize I was
holding. As Burns' emergency contact and the
closest thing to next of kin, I get the feeling that
Cindy can tell me Burns' status, but that doesn't
mean Burns doesn't want them to keep certain
things quiet, which is what I suspect.

"Thank you, Clint," Cindy sighs with relief.

"Don't worry about it. Bye Cindy."

"Thanks again Clint. Bye," Cindy says before
hanging up the phone.

I am down the stairs crossing my parking lot
feeling wound up, tension building between my
shoulders with every step. The chance to see
Dawn is exciting, but the memory of our last
encounter is still fresh in my mind. Burns and the
possibility of his declining health makes me
uneasy.

If Luke could see me now, he'd give me shit
over my avoidance. *How many giants get nervous when
they have to confront a tiny beauty and an elderly old man?*

Only a few cars are parked outside Benny's
tonight but it's still early. I can hear the classic 90s
country music playing from Benny's old juke box
before I even cross the street. A few years back

Burns fixed the juke box for Benny. Well as best he could—ever since, you can't play anything from The Judds. Knowing Burns that may have been on purpose. He never liked them.

Burns' voice carries through the front door before I walk in. He is sitting at the bar with Dawn who has an unguarded smile on her face. The smile is so full of sweetness my teeth ache, and it stops me in my tracks. I have never seen Dawn like this. Granted this is only my third encounter with her but seeing her smile like this is intoxicating. Even Burns looks mesmerized by her while he chats her ear off.

Pulling my phone out to call Cindy, I let her know I have found Burns safe and sound. "That's a relief," Cindy sighs. "Do you want me to come get him?"

"Yeah. But, give it an hour."

"I don't think that's a good idea."

"I'll keep an eye on him," I promise. Reluctantly, Cindy agrees, and we hang up. Knowing her, she will be here in forty-five minutes. That doesn't give me a long time to convince the stubborn Burns that he needs to leave soon. Having a pretty face like Dawn giving him her full attention will not help either.

"What were they doing in there?" I hear Dawn ask, engrossed in Burns' story, as I make my way to the bar. My imposing frame cannot be ignored for long. She briefly glances my way. Her eyes grow large with surprise before the unguarded brilliance of her smile turns polite. It is the kind of smile you give to a customer and not at all the smile I had hoped for.

"The boys were looking for bicycle parts, but it was too dark, and they were too little to scavenge. After wandering the yard, Jax climbs up a pile of stacked crushed cars. None of his brothers even noticed! Jax is such a sweet boy, but he had no fear and was a wild little thing. He kept his brothers on their toes," Burns shares with a mischievous smile and warmth in his eyes.

He may have acted put out by us Colson boys to our faces, but deep down I know he cared for us like we were his own sons.

"Telling stories are we, Burns?" I tease patting him on the back. "Cindy has been looking all over for you."

"Bring Clint a beer will you, Sweetness—"

I snap my head up. *Sweetness?* Did he just call her *Sweetness?* That is my thing! I feel the heat rush to my face.

"—and then I'll tell you the rest of the story," he finishes.

"As you wish," Dawn says with a smile only for the old man.

A pang of jealousy flares in the pit of my stomach, but I push it away. *Seriously, am I going to be jealous over an old man?*

"Don't worry. I know you called dibs," Burns whispers with a wink as she leaves.

"One drink only. Then you go home with Cindy when she gets here," I say, ignoring Burns' comment. "And stop calling her Sweetness."

"Jealous?" Burns wiggles his eyebrows.

"And no funny business."

"Why, Clint, I'm hurt," he says as Dawn returns with my beer. "For that, I will tell Dawn all about your run in with the law."

"You're impossible," I say, accepting my beer from Dawn. Our hands touch sending those tingles up my arm. The look on Dawn's face tells me she feels it too. She pulls away not meeting my eye. Disappointment settles in my stomach like a brick.

"Burns, let me check on the others," she mumbles and slips away from the bar heading for three guys playing pool in the back. Walking slowly, she looks uncomfortable, even a little cautious, as if not to provoke. Keeping a large gap between the men and herself, she asks if they want anything. After they give their orders, she slips away like a ghost.

"She's a frightened little thing," Burns comments only loud enough for me to hear as she fills up a pitcher for her customers.

"She seems comfortable around you," I retort.

"Don't you worry, Clint. She'll come around. I have a nose for these things," he says pointing to his nose before snorting into his glass.

"Now where was I, *Sweetness*?" he asks with a smirk turning towards Dawn as she returns. I wish he would stop calling her that. She slips close to Burns over the other side of the bar. If she had her way, I bet she would prefer to be invisible. "Oh, right! Jax. He climbs up on a pile of crushed cars when Eric realizes he's gone. The boys are making all kinds of ruckus now. They wake me up and I am thinking, *where is my damned dog.*"

As Dawn leans over, her baggy V-neck shirt opens wide before my eyes revealing a black satin bra. I am a goner in less than three seconds flat! My pants become too tight. My dick grows large in my pants, and it presses up against my zipper. Making matters worse, she folds her arms on the bar, pushing her breasts together. I nearly lose it. I have to look away. Her creamy skin and sexy bra are turning me into a teenage boy. It takes everything I have to look at Burns—nothing like looking at his wrinkled profile to kill a hard on.

"When I go out to see what the hell is going on, I see little Jax watching his brothers run around looking for him while he sits up there like he's King of the Hill." Burns finishes his story, looking happier than I have seen in a long time.

"Your dog didn't chase the boys off?" she asks, glancing at me with her shy smile.

I return the smile thankful she didn't catch me looking down her shirt. I cannot stop myself, and I glance a few more times, not helping my situation downstairs.

"No, she was following Eric around," he says. "He always had a way with animals."

"People not so much," I mutter with a wink to Dawn.

Her smile falters as she straightens, taking away the beautiful view and turning slightly as she shifts all her attention to Burns.

I never cared that others have found me to be unnerving. My large size and scary disposition are part of who I am. But, if I scare Dawn, that bothers me. I don't want to frighten her.

"Eric is moody, but has a good heart," Burns admits before taking a drink from his beer. Dawn's focus is still only on the old man. She wipes the surrounding area because his shaking hands cause a mess and reminds me why I am here.

"All my boys have good hearts." Burns tacks on.

Guilt hits me like a ton of bricks. Burns never had kids of his own. We were the closest thing he had to children of his own, and since I lost my part time help, my visits with Burns have been less frequent. With Luke back, him and I are probably Burns' only visitors. It never dawned on me the old man was lonely until now.

"How about one more beer?" I ask Burns before taking a big gulp of my own nearly full beer. "But you have to promise to go with Cindy without a fuss when she gets here."

"Make it two and you have a deal." Burns extends his hand—*the shady bastard*.

"Deal." I return the shake before turning my attention to Dawn who has been silent during our entire exchange.

"Can we get another round?" I ask. She turns away but looks over her shoulder at me with a smile. My heart quickens. I watch Dawn walk to the tap with her tight ass looking beyond amazing in black skinny jeans. It forces me to make more adjustments to my already tight bulge.

"She isn't like them other girls," Burns whispers, with narrowed eyes. His fierce gaze is a silent warning.

"I know." I admit before draining the rest of my beer. Dawn is definitely not like the other girls I am use too. She doesn't seem to be interested in anyone, preferring to make herself as invisible as possible. "Don't worry. She seems to only have eyes for you."

"Darn right!" Burns winks with a big toothy smile. "I still got it."

"What do you still got?" Dawn asks, placing our beer before us. Her voice is so low I can barely hear it, and I wonder if she even meant to say it out loud.

"My charm, Sweetness," he says without skipping a beat.

Damn it! Will he stop calling her that already! Now it's just getting annoying.

"Too much charm and too much time if you ask me," she replies with a smile that could brighten my world during its darkest hour. I like seeing her like this, unguarded and talkative like she was at the grocery store. Whatever has caused the sadness in her eyes hasn't broken her, but it sure is doing its best to drown her.

"Then it's good I didn't ask you." He playfully pats her hand before picking up his beer. His hand trembles, spilling beer down the sides. Grabbing the towel she left by Burns, Dawn mops up the counter, and for once I see something other than fear or sadness cross her face. I see concern.

"I think I need to cut you off Burns," she hesitates, her eyes swiftly sliding my way before settling back to Burns. She adds, "Plus Clint looks tired."

"Oh, he's fine." Burns shrugs. "He owes me one more. Then I'll leave."

"I have got to work early tomorrow so drink up."

"Work, work, work," Burns grumbles, guilt sucker-punching me in the stomach again. The old man knows how to lay it on thick.

"You want to come in and help?" I ask hoping to redeem my absence. "I could use another part-time person."

"Can't handle the shop on your own?" he challenges, giving Dawn a wink. She is relaxing the more she watches the two of us banter back and forth.

"I can handle the shop on my own." I pause to drink my beer before adding, "But I understand if you don't want to help."

"I never said I wouldn't help." He puts down his beer glass into a small puddle of beer. Dawn is quick to clean things up.

"It's okay. I know you're jealous that I'm a better mechanic," I reply, hoping Burns doesn't notice Dawn and I assessing him like trained medical professionals.

"Jealous! Ha!" Burns retorts. "Taught you everything you know. Him and his brothers had me going gray early in life. Aged me ten years with all their shenanigans."

"You age well, like a fine wine," Dawn compliments before walking away to clean up after her customers that just left.

Knowing we will be leaving soon, I realize she will be alone at Benny's, and that doesn't sit well.

"I think I will stick around until closing," I say more to myself than to Burns who snorts into his beer glass.

"I doubt she would like that much," Burns says patting my shoulder. "But don't worry, I can help with that!"

"Please don't," I grumble under my breath, knowing full well that Burns will stick his nose where it doesn't belong.

Dawn returns, putting the dirty dishes into the bin.

"Anyone coming to help you close up?" Burns asks, turning to give me a not so subtle wink.

"Alfred is coming by later after we close to clean up the kitchen. He has to take his wife to work," she shares with a nervousness tremble in her voice.

I don't have to be a mind reader to know she isn't comfortable being here alone.

"I'll stay here until you close up, Sweetness," Burns says, and I groan. The bastard is doing it on purpose now. He knows he got under my skin.

"You know Cindy is on her way here." I sigh, knowing Burns will claim chivalry isn't dead and stall all attempts to leave.

"I'll be fine. I think you should go with Cindy before she has you locked up at night," she says, trying to convince him to leave with Cindy much to my relief.

"I'll stay and help with the trash, if it's all right with you?" I offer.

Dawn eyes me while biting her bottom lip looking unsure. The move is sexy as hell, and it triggers all kinds of sizzling thoughts. Like me reaching underneath her hair and grabbing the back of neck while sucking on her bottom lip. I could almost feel her press up against me and hear her moan. I snap back to reality hoping Burns isn't watching too carefully, while I adjust my constant hard on.

"Alfred will take care of the trash," she tries to justify, but her uncertainty straightens my spine with hope.

I don't think she wanted to decline my offer.

"I didn't see your car out there," I point out. "Did the battery die again?"

"Yes…" Her words trail off as she starts biting that lip again. "I have your coat. I forgot to give it back."

"How do you plan on getting home?" I narrow my eyes at her, ignoring her attempt to change the subject.

"I'll walk," she admits, looking as if that tidbit of information cost her.

"I'll give you a ride or I'll walk with you."

"No. It's fine."

"Let the boy walk you home," Burns says eyeing the two of us, "It will be the most action he's seen in a while."

"Old Man. I'm not afraid to call Miss Janet," I threaten before draining the rest of my beer.

"Miss Janet?" Dawn asks, eyeing Burns and I with an amused smile.

I can tell she is relieved the focus isn't on her anymore.

"She has a thing for me," Burns confesses, and I cannot stop my snort of laughter knowing what is coming next. "But no one believes me."

"More like a plot to kill you," I retort with a laugh. "He's right. No one believes him. Several years back, he tried to prove his theory and showed up at Miss Janet's house hoping for some action."

"I'm telling you. I was close to wooing her if it wasn't for widowed Mrs. Bartley and her gossiping hens," Burns mutters, looking annoyed.

I have turned the table on him, revealing his embarrassing stories. "Mrs. Bartley and her 'gossiping hens'—" I say, air quoting gossiping hens.

As Dawn leans in engrossed by the story, her shirt opens wide again, sending heat rushing to pool in my pants, and nearly choking me. I try to continue. "They wa-warned Miss Janet that Burns was only after a bit of tail. Miss Janet, being hot tempered, nearly took Burns' head off with a frying pan."

"No!" she laughs patting Burns' hand. "Cock blocked by gossiping hens."

"Supposedly Miss Janet has been out for blood ever since." I finish my story leaning in closer to Dawn loving her attention for once and taking in her delicious scent. I could pick her out of a line up blindfolded as long as I could get close enough to smell her scent.

"See no one believes me!" Burns grumbles before getting up from the stool. Holding on tight to the bar, it's hard to tell if it's a dizzy spell or intoxication that has him a little wobbly on his feet.

"Let's get you home, Old Man," I say unable to mask the worry in my voice.

I quickly call Cindy, who is already on her way, because Burns has me concerned with his unsteadiness.

"Let me help you," I say as I throw down some cash on the bar before offering my hand, but he pushes it away.

"I'm fine," Burns mutters, sending me his signature glare. "You're as bad as Cindy."

"That stings Old Man." I put my hand to my heart, fixing him with what I hope is a wounded look.

"I'll help you Burns," Dawn offers, coming around from the bar. Her mouthwatering aroma trailing in her wake. I swear I can taste her on my tongue.

"Thank you, *Sweetness*." Burns' smiles before sticking his tongue at me.

The bastard!

"Watch out. He'll cop a feel," I grumble, following them to the door.

"Burns. You wouldn't dare!" Dawn says, scandalized.

"I would," Burns admits, patting her arm as she leads him outside.

Cindy is out of her car holding the front passenger door open. Dawn helps Burns get into the car before leaning down, giving him a quick peck on the cheek. "Try not to give Cindy too much crap."

"Giving her crap is the highlight of my day," Burns says with a smile. "Take care, Dawn."

Together Dawn and I watch Cindy drive off before heading back into the bar.

"Can I get you something to drink?" she asks awkwardly bringing a smile to my face.

"Sure. Water," I answer, sounding more confident.

Nodding, Dawn holds my stare for a moment before turning to grab a fresh glass. I ogle her backside unapologetically knowing no one is around to call me out on it. When she turns around and slides the water and a straw my way, I lean in to take in her scent. It's my drug of choice.

"What's it like to have brothers? Three, right?" Dawn asks, breaking the growing silence. Hesitantly, she leans up against the counter careful not to get too close.

Knowing I have her full attention, I don't sneak a peek at her black satin bra. It tests my restraint, and I cannot help but feel a little proud of myself.

"Yep. Three, and it was chaotic," I respond, "Do you have siblings?"

"No, I was an only child," she shares, and I get the feeling that by her sudden stiffness, she regrets sharing something personal about herself. I learned my lesson. I shouldn't press Dawn too hard. She is quick to close herself off, but I want to know more about her.

"It's not so bad," I say, getting back to the question of my brothers. "I always have someone to help me move."

"That's convenient," she says with a small smile. She holds my stare a little longer than normal.

My attention seems to make her uncomfortable, but I cannot help myself. I could get lost in her eyes despite the sadness. They infatuate me.

"You know about my family. What is yours like?" I ask, immediately regretting it. Her smile fades as she builds up her walls again.

"I should clean up. Closing time is soon." Dawn avoids the question. "Do you want anything else?"

"Let me help you," I blurt out a little too desperate to keep her attention.

"I can handle things," she sighs as sadness replaces the fear in her eyes once more.

"I don't doubt it, but I have nothing better to do," I return. "I promise I won't ask you anymore personal questions."

"Oh…" she trails off. I called her out and now she doesn't know how to react. Looking a mixture of scared and annoyed, she turns and leaves me at the bar. Heading for the tables she lifts the chairs up onto the tables.

Walking over to her, I help, but say nothing. If she doesn't want me to help, she can tell me herself. I know that I am pushing my luck, but something tells me she needs to be pushed. I know there are guys out there that live off drama, and Dawn definitely has drama, but I'm not like that. Part of me doesn't care if I ever know what plagues her as long as it doesn't make her look so sad all the time.

"Where too?" I ask after we finished closing the bar down.

"Not far," she says, locking the front door and tucking the keys into my coat. She had tried to give it to me before we left, but I refused to take it. Her flimsy jacket is not enough to keep her warm while walking home.

"I can give you a ride."

"I live a block and a half behind the bar. Next to Amber," she says turning to face me. A look of determination on her face. "Sarah and Amber say this is the safest place around," Dawn throws at me. It's hard to read her face in the semi darkness of the night.

"Are you trying to get rid of me?" I ask.

"If it's the safest place, I think I'll be okay walking home."

"Maybe so, but I would still feel better knowing you made it home safe and sound," I reply, walking up to her.

I tower over her. It is the first time we have stood this close together since the store. Her brown sugar and vanilla scent invade my nostrils, and it takes everything I have not to pull her close and breath in.

"I doubt that I can convince you otherwise," she notes, looking up at me with those bewitching blue eyes.

I don't respond, but nod.

"You are just as stubborn as Burns," she accuses.

The autumn air whistles past, sending Dawn's hair flying around her face. She pulls it quickly into a bun. I am struck again by her beauty as she laughs at herself and the frenzy of the weather.

"I'm this way." She points toward the back of the building, and I follow unsure what to say. Silence again descends between us. It isn't an awkward silence, but a comfortable one, as if we both realize that we can be comfortable together in silence.

It is too dark for us to enjoy the scenery as we walk, but all the same, it is peaceful. The moon is just a sliver in the night sky, but the stars are out and bright. Autumn is in the air. The temperature has changed from the heat of August to the cooling of September.

All too soon, we are standing before her front door.

"What did Benny say about the battery?" I ask, hoping to prolong our time together.

"I haven't told him yet," she admits. Her front porch light is not bright enough for me to see her face well enough to read what I think is hesitation.

"Are you worried about telling him?"

"No... should I be?"

"No. I can get your battery replaced tomorrow," I tell her, as a plan begins to form in my mind. With a little help from Burns, I might be able to get Dawn to let her guard down long enough to let me help her. "But I'll need a favor from you."

"What kind of favor?" she asks. I can hear her uncertainty.

"Have brunch with Burns and me tomorrow morning," I tell her, nervousness tickling my stomach. *Brunch? Since when do I do brunch?*

"I don't know." She sounds close to rejecting my offer.

"Don't make me beg." I take a step closer to her. She reacts and takes a step up the stairs leading to her front door. She is close to eye level now. "It will make Burns happy, and he needs to get out and go somewhere other than to a bar."

"I have to work tomorrow."

"I'll get you home before you have to go in." I reassure her, taking another step closer. She steps up another stair. Now she can look me straight in the eye. I cannot see the bewitching blue, but I can see a longing and a hint of desire that sparks some heat in my pants. My hands itch to touch Dawn's hip, wrap around her waist and pull her into my chest.

"I think you should beg," Dawn whispers to my surprise. She starts to lean forward closing the small gap between us before catching herself and taking the final step up the stairs.

"Please." I smile from ear to ear. I am so close to getting her to say yes.

"Ok."

"Ok?"

"Yes. Ok," she repeats with a smile that could be my undoing, but I am too excited to care about the power she has over me, because she said *yes*.

"I'll pick you up at 10:00."

"Night, Clint." She waves and turns for the door.

"Night, Dawn." I call back before turning to leave, the biggest fucking smile on my face.

6

- Dawn -

"What the hell is brunch?" Burns asks sounding put out as we walk into Sugar and Sweet Bakery. Immediately the smells recall memories of my mother in our old apartment, baking one of her old recipes. Sometimes it is difficult to recall my mother's face, but then a smell will trigger a vision and I will see her again in my mind in vivid details; the way she would fish bone braid her golden-brown hair; the smile that never faltered even when one of her experimental baking creations turned into a disastrous mess; the splash of freckles across her nose and cheeks. It is hard to believe that it has been almost ten years since she passed away. The thought of her passing hurts less; yet, it still can be suffocating at times.

Sugar and Sweet Bakery is painted floor to ceiling in pinks, purples and yellows. Burns is turned off by the charming bakery, scowling at the small white wrought-iron tables with matching wrought-iron chairs sprinkled around. In every empty spot, there is a shelf or end table holding vases of flowers and antique tea pots. I picture my grandmother's home looking like this. I love it instantly.

"Take a seat, Old Man," Clint growls from behind as we settle around a small table.

"Are you growing a pussy, Clint?" Burns says a little too loudly. "You brought us to a girly shop."

"It's a bakery, Burns." Clint stifles a laugh. "It's smells delicious in here."

"If you say so, but I'm not drinking that sugary shit they call coffee. I'll have mine black," he grumbles.

Burns brightened up when he opened his door and found me looking back at him, but turned into a bear when we told him we were taking him to brunch. *Who doesn't like brunch?* Burns apparently. It took a lot of begging from Clint and I before he agreed.

All night, I wondered about the two. They seem close yet share no physical features. Burns is short with a friendly face and bright smile. Clint is large, black-haired, with cool piercing blue eyes. His appearance is menacing, and even his smile is petrifying. A scar puckers one side of his mouth as if in a permanent snarl, yet I am becoming unfazed by it. I wonder how he got that scar, and after watching him handle the men that gave Amber a hard time the other night, I can't image the scar was the result of Clint starting any kind of trouble. The two men have similar mannerisms though, as if they have spent years together. They both have the same glower when they don't like something. Burns' glare could rival anyone. I see where Clint gets his from. And, they both walk with a confidence I wish I could have.

Clint takes off his navy-blue work jacket, revealing another Colson Auto Body Shop shirt underneath. Warmth rushes through my body. I want to fan my face. His body is amazing! His arm muscles are on full display in the brightly lit bakery. Everything is so dim at Benny's that I really hadn't noticed the subtle hard lines in Clint's face or how toned his muscles are. There is a brightness to his blue eyes, that make him look intense, scary and smoldering all at the same time. The bakery is already warm, and the heat I feel just looking at Clint turns into a burn that spreads like fire throughout my entire body.

Forget coffee, I need a cold glass of water!

We make our way to the counter showcasing lines of baked goods. My mouth waters in anticipation.

"There is so much to choose from," I say, glancing up at Clint who is gazing at me.

"What?" I ask.

"I haven't seen you smile like this before," he admits, his terrifying smile spreading across his face.

A blush is quick to heat my face as I drop the smile and glance away hoping he doesn't notice. I knew I should not have accepted Clint's offer, but the loneliness was wearing on me, and somehow Clint has this gentleness about him that relaxes me, despite his spine-chilling presence. It's hard to say *no* to him.

"Can I help you two?" the bakery clerk squeaks from behind the case, growing a little pale when she looks at Clint.

"Two black coffees and whatever the lady wants," Clint responds while I browse through the selection.

"Get one of everything if you can't decide," he adds.

"I couldn't, possibly," I say as my stomach growls, betraying me.

Clint laughs quietly as he glances at my stomach. Then his eyes roam over me and it sends tingles throughout my body. *This was such a bad idea!*

For so long, I felt so apart from the world, bouncing from foster home to foster home. It was not until I was on my own, working in a bakery much like this one, that I dared to step out of my comfort zone and tried to reconnect with the world. That is when I really let Dain into my life, and my heart. Then, he abandoned me, and I was forced to close myself off again. It was easy stepping back into a lonely existence. It is harder staying there. Clint's subtle pushing makes it hard to turn him down. He makes it hard to want to be invisible because being seen with Clint brings attention my way. Not bad attention, but attention none the less.

"Have you decided what you want?" the lady asks reminding me that I am staring at Clint who is smirking down at me.

"Yes. I'd like the large chocolate brownie with a caramel latte."

"Burns will be so disappointed in you," Clint whispers in my ear while he reaches in his back pocket for his wallet.

"Last I checked I wasn't a *man* so I think I can get away with it," I whisper back pulling my wallet out to pay.

"Put it away. I've got this," he says, laying his hand over my own. His hand is massive, and his touch surprises me at first. I have made great strides getting used to not having physical contact with others. These days, being touched by most people sets me on edge, but Clint's touch sends tingles through me. Relaxing a little, I put my wallet back letting him pay.

Comparing Clint to those around him is not possible. There are not many who can come close to his size. I have never felt so tiny standing next to someone. Others fear him, I can see that in the way they peer at him when he isn't looking. Their expressions wide-eyed. Maybe I should also fear him too but seeing him with Burns—the way he cares about the old man—makes me see him as a gentle giant.

"I have got the next round," I sigh, grabbing my coffee and brownie.

"So, I get a next time?" Clint winks at me as we head back to the table, causing another blush to flood my face.

"About damn time," Burns mumbles snatching up his coffee. "It's black coffee. It shouldn't take so long."

"Sorry, Burns, I couldn't decide what to get," I confess, pushing my brownie towards him. "Help me eat this?"

"That's what happens when they give you too many damn choices. You can't figure out what you want, and everyone is left waiting."

"Someone is in a foul mood," I observe, taking a bite of the brownie. As delicious as it is it doesn't compare to the brownies my mother use to make. "Have a bite. I bet it'll make you feel better."

"You're just trying to sweeten me up," Burns states though he sounds less annoyed.

"Oh, come on, old man. Don't be so grumpy." Clint shoves his hands over his hair. His hair is pulled back today, making him look younger. His beard is getting longer too.

I want to rub my hand against his check to see if his beard is soft. It looks soft.

"I'm sorry. I won't ever take you to brunch again," he chides.

"Boy, if I had a nickel for every time you told me you were sorry, I could *maybe* pay for the fancy overpriced coffee they serve in this joint," Burns spits back.

"Complaining about nonsense, Burns?" a lady not much younger than Burns asks as she approaches our table. She's dressed like a Kennedy. Her hair and make-up are perfect. She is too fancy and out of place in this cozy bakery.

"You'd know, being the queen of complaining," Burns retorts bitterly. Crossing his arms, he shifts away from the woman. "Where are your pecking hens? Busy being in everyone's business?"

"I have no idea who you are referring too," the lady says, looking angry but still holding that polite tone.

There is bad blood between these two, I think.

"Probably out having *brunch* spreading vicious rumors," Burns mutters rolling his eyes.

When did he turn twelve? I wonder, flashing an amused smile at Clint who looks equally entertained.

"Clint who's your friend?" the lady asks, looking at me, assessing me. This is not the attention I want.

"Mrs. Bartley, this is Dawn. Benny and Linda's niece." Clint introduces us, and I shake her hand recalling Burns story from last night.

"Is Miss Janet coming... to brunch?" I blurt out to Mrs. Bartley.

Burns sits up straighter, glancing over to the door. For Burns, I'd risk a little bad attention. He is as lonely as me, and it's nice having a friend, even if that friend might land you in a whole heap of trouble.

"Not likely, if she knows Burns is here," Mrs. Bartley taunts, observing Burns' sudden interest in the entrance. "I should be off to warn her."

"Please don't. I would hate to miss the opportunity to meet *the* Miss Janet," I exclaim, noticing that Burns and Clint are eyeing me in a funny way.

"Miss Janet?" Mrs. Bartley asks with narrowed eyes.

"I told Dawn that Miss Janet makes the best cherry pie, and Dawn has been eager to meet her," Clint throws in, coming to my aide. *The man is observant.*

Not meaning to, my hand slips across Clint's muscular thigh and squeezes it. The touch alone is innocent, but the way his eyes darken, send heat rushing to my core, and butterflies soaring around my chest.

"Miss Janet," Burns says loudly, and snaps my attention back from my internal reaction to Clint. I don't think he meant to call out to her but all the same, a lovely little woman around the same age as Burns shuffles over to us. She looks at home here in the bakery. It was likely her choice to meet here. She does not have the political wife vibe that Mrs. Bartley has, but more of a retired librarian look about her with her silver hair in a bun, oversized glasses and sweater.

"Burns. I'm surprised to see you here," she comments before looking around at us all, smiling sweetly. I love her immediately, even if she did try to take Burns out with a frying pan. *He probably deserved it anyway.*

"Here sit down." Burns offers his chair to Miss Janet. Despite the muttered protests from Mrs. Bartley, Miss Janet takes a seat. Once she is seated, Burns pushes Clint out of his chair and plops down. "Can I get you anything?"

"Tea would be nice."

"You heard the lady. Get her some tea," Burns orders Clint, shooing him off.

I bite back a laugh as I watch him head for the counter smiling back at me.

"Where should I sit?" Mrs. Bartley asks, eyeing my spot.

"Anywhere but at this table," Burns quips. "Miss Janet would you like some of Dawn's brownie?"

And just like that, Burns takes away my brownie, pushing it towards Miss Janet. I might need to rethink this friendship.

"Don't mind if I do," she says, snatching up a fork.

"What about Brunch?" Mrs. Bartley protests in one more attempt to lure Miss Janet away from Burns.

"I'll only be a moment," Miss Janet replies between bites of my brownie. "This is delicious. Thank you, Burns."

"No problem," he coos, having eyes only for the great Miss Janet.

Mrs. Bartley finally turns to leave. She takes up a table closer to the entrance and as far away from us as possible.

"Why don't Dawn and I leave you two," Clint suggests, placing Miss Janet's tea before her.

I glance up at him and he nods towards the entrance. A nervous excitement tickles my stomach.

"You two have fun," Burns says, still not taking his eyes off Miss Janet.

I hold my laughter in until we exit Sugar and Sweet. I turn towards Clint who snatches up my hands in his. "Looks like Miss Janet *does* have a thing for Burns," I giggle.

"I know I'll never hear the end of it now," Clint admits as we glance inside at the couple enjoying my brownie.

Clint's hands are warm, and his large frame blocks the autumn wind. I shiver from the cold because I wore my old jean jacket. I couldn't muster up enough courage to wear Clint's coat that is laying on my bed. "They are rather cute together," I observe before glancing over at Mrs. Bartley who is eyeing Clint and I with a raised eyebrow and a scowl that must be permanently plastered on her face. "And it looks like I made my first enemy."

"Mrs. Bartley is harmless but watch out for that vicious tongue of hers." Clint notes, squeezing my hands.

I suddenly realize how close we are to one another. My heartbeat picks up. I like this closeness, but it isn't a good idea. I will crave more of it, and with a future that is unclear, I am not ready to risk hurting my already bruised heart. Clint frowns at me as I step back away from him.

After several seconds pass, he asks, "Do you mind taking a walk?"

"I'm fond of walking," I let slip. My gut clenches at my carelessness.

Jerking his head over his shoulder in the direction he wants to go in, we start our walk.

Silence falls between us. Our stroll is slow. I don't know how Clint's long legs can maintain my slower pace. His hands are shoved deep into his pockets. His shoulders are hunched over. I watch the faces of the people as they pass by us. Many eye me with curiosity before shifting their glances away when they realize I am with Clint.

"Everyone is scared of you," I blurt out when another wide-eyed bystander takes a second look as we pass.

"My dad wasn't well liked around here," he shrugs glancing around. "I look like him."

"I look like my dad," I admit, looking down at my shoes. "At least that is what my mom always said."

Silence whirls around us again. Our slow stroll moves us away from Peak Valley's downtown with its small, closely connected shops to a large open area of land. Playground equipment, picnic tables, benches, tennis and basketball courts sit within a circular walking path. It reminds me of the park my mother used to take me too when I was younger.

The aroma of coffee pulls my attention toward a food truck advertising specialty coffees and pastries several feet from us. "Can I buy you a coffee?" I ask.

"As long as this doesn't count as my next time," Clint responds. He winks. His hand finds the small of my back as he leads me toward the food truck, and I like the feel of it. The warmth it gives, the feelings it stirs within me. The idea of belonging to someone doesn't seem so bad when I think of belonging to Clint.

"Deal." I smile up at him, absorbing the familiar tingles that zip through my body. I step up to the counter, pleased to see they have a caramel latte and a brownie. Clint orders his coffee black and only moves his hand from my lower back to hold my latte and brownie while I pay.

"Would you like some?" I offer a bite to Clint, holding my brownie up towards his mouth. Clint leans forward taking a small bite. Clint watches my lips with his chilly blue eyes. They darken into a stormy gray as his pupils dilate. A full body blush, starting from my face works its way down, heating up my body. Sweat beads along my backbone.

"Thank you," Clint mumbles, color tinting his own cheeks.

"How do you know Burns?" I ask. Picturing the old man cools the desire Clint has ignited in my awakening body.

"After my mom died and my dad checked out on life, Burns made sure my brothers and I did nothing stupid." Clint says as he breaks off our eye contact and walks again. Briefly glancing back at me, he adds with a wink, "Luke was a lost cause though."

"I will share that with Amber," I laugh. Seeing a bench a few feet away, I add, "Can we rest for a while?"

"Are you ok?" Clint asks, concern in his eyes. He takes a seat so close our thighs are touching.

Maybe sitting wasn't a good idea. The familiar tingles zing up and down my leg.

"I'm fine." I reply, brushing off his concern, not wanting to explain my tiredness. I peer into my coffee, not sure how to steer our conversation into safer waters, and ask "What does your dad do?"

"I'll make you a deal." Clint drapes his arm around the back of the bench, a mischievous glint in his eye, tickling a smile out of me. "A question for a question."

"Question for a question," I repeat. My heart falls to my stomach as panic bubbles. "I don't know."

"You don't have to answer anything you don't want to," he reassures me. I can feel the heaviness of his stare, but avoid it, looking out over the park. I put myself in this situation, asking Clint about his life. It is only fair to give back, and I want to know more about the gentle giant that scares everyone, but me.

"Deal," I say, pushing away all thoughts about why this isn't a good idea. I lean into Clint's arm for more warmth.

"My dad is dead," Clint answers quickly with no remorse. "He drank himself to death two years after I graduated from high school."

"I'm sorry." The words come out on their own, and I mentally kick myself. Those same two words that I am tired of hearing when people hear my sad story slip out, and I say them to Clint.

"He isn't worth a second thought." Clint shrugs. His arm that is laying across the back of the bench curls around my shoulder. I am unable to hold back a smile. Clint tenses as he stares down at me. Swallowing hard, he asks, "What does your dad do?"

"Never knew my dad." I shrug, taking a sip of my coffee. I can still feel his eyes on me.

"Who took care of you after your mom died?"

"I went into foster care." I shrug again. Tension builds up at the base of my neck.

"How come you didn't come live with Benny and Linda?"

"That is your third question," I point out rolling my shoulders. This was a bad idea. Too many truths are uncovering all my lies. I need to steer us in another direction because not answering that question will only make Clint more curious. He pulls his arm back to rest on the bench again. I look back into those fierce blue eyes and smile despite my unsettled feelings about opening myself up to Clint.

"What did you do to get in trouble with the law?" I ask.

"Pulling out the big guns," Clint comments, sucking in a deep breath before letting it out slowly. "The Sheriff tried to pin a stolen engine from my high school principal's truck on me."

"A stolen engine?" My eyebrows scrunch in confusion.

"Principal Smith accused my brother Jax of stealing the engine after he refused to let my brother walk at graduation for his senior prank," Clint explains with a ghost of a smile on his face.

"When Jax's alibi checked out, Smith went after me. I was in school to be a mechanic."

"Did you do it?" I ask, narrowing my eyes at my gentle giant.

He looks guilty as his smile widens across his intense yet handsome face. "My classmates and teachers vouched for me. I was in Kansas City. There was no way it could have been me." He winks down at me, looking smug.

"Do you know who did it?" I question, not convinced Clint wasn't involved.

"I suspect Burns." Clint presses his lips together holding back a laugh.

"No!" I cry out in disbelief.

"He gave Principal Smith a discount on a used engine and threw in free labor." Clint continues. It is getting hard for him to hold back his laughter. "I'm willing to bet my truck that the *used* engine Burns put in was Principal Smith's stolen engine."

Feeling the rumble of laughter escape Clint is contagious. Both of us break out into a fit of laughter. Leaning into each other, his arm curls tightly around my shoulder as butterflies erupt in my chest. Tears of laughter blur my vision. When one escapes, Clint's thumb brushes it away. Our laughter dies with the sudden shift in emotion. The look in his eyes send a shiver through me. It is a dark and needy look that is so enticing, but I cannot give into it. I need to navigate us away from it.

"Why would Burns steal the engine?" I ask.

Clearing his throat, Clint answers, still staring deep into my eyes with a grin that sends more tingles down my body straight to my woman parts, "To pull the heat off of Jax for his senior prank."

"Did it work?" I ask. I bite my lip hoping he cannot see how much his closeness is turning me on.

"He still didn't get to walk at graduation, but the Sheriff stopped trying to pin trespassing charges on Jax." Clint says.

His thumb pulls my lip from my teeth causing me to gasp.

"That must have been some prank," I whisper, wondering if he will kiss me.

"He shrink-wrapped the school," Clint leans in closer. "My turn."

"Your turn?" I ask confused because all I can think about is his lips and how close they are getting to mine.

"My turn to ask a question." He has a smug smile that shows off his perfect white teeth.

"Right. Your turn," I breathe out.

"Were you ever in trouble with the law?" He raises his brows playfully, and with just one question my anticipation turns sour in my stomach.

"No," I lie, pulling away from Clint, tearing my eyes off of his lips, and looking away. I should not have agreed to play Clint's one-for-one game. It's not like me to take unnecessary risks, but since I have moved to Peak Valley, I keep taking one after the other, usually involving Clint.

I take a sip of my latte. It tastes as cold and bitter as I feel.

Amanda Lee Dixon

7

- Clint -

"You have never been to a festival?" I ask, shaking my head in disbelief. We climb out of my truck. "What about a carnival?"

"Just the ones they had at school." Dawn shrugs then asks, "Does that count?"

"No. It doesn't count," I scoff. "It's settled. I'm taking you to Peak Valley's Fall Festival."

"You are?" Dawn's bewitching blue eyes swivel my way.

All morning, I have been lost in her eyes. I fought against the instinct to hold her hand. For a few moments, she let me touch her, but most of the time, she shied away. Overall, she seemed to relax a little, though there were a few moments when she would build those walls up, but they were weak at best. If I am lucky, I might get her to hang out with me more.

"It would be un-American not too." I grin and gently nudge her shoulder as we trek across the parking lot to the grocery store.

"When is this Fall Festival?"

"Next weekend."

"I might have to work," she frowns.

"Ask for a day off," I say with a shrug, hoping she doesn't try to come up with excuses not to go, or flat reject me like she did last time. Before she can respond, the automatic doors open, and we enter the grocery store. Grabbing a cart, I ask, "Why are we here again? Didn't you just buy groceries?"

"Quit your whining." Dawn sends me a playful smile. "I need chocolate chips."

"What are you making?" I lean in to let her sugary scent fill my nose. At any opportunity to get in close, I take it and inhale her in.

"Double chocolate chip cookies," she replies twirling a strand of hair. I notice she does that when she is distracted by her thoughts.

She looks up, over her shoulder at me with that beautiful smile, and I fight the urge to kiss her. I remember her looking nervous and biting her lip. Since picking her up this morning, I have not stopped thinking about kissing those lips, and now I need to know if those lips taste as good as she smells.

"Are these cookies for me?" I ask, still staring at her lips. "You know, to *thank* me."

"Maybe. If Burns doesn't eat them all." She laughs when I narrow my eyes at her. *Damn old man!*

"All he will eat is Miss Janet's cherry pie," I grumble, pushing the cart towards the baking aisle. Glancing back, I catch Dawn checking me out, her eyes skimming over my backside before landing on my smug smile. *Hell Yeah!* Her cheeks flush with color. Looking down at her feet, she rushes to catch up.

"You'll enjoy the Fall Festival. A lot of the locals bring baked goods for sale," I tell her because I plan to take her even if I have to talk to Benny myself about giving her a day off. Hell, I am not even opposed to enlisting Burns' help. I would owe him, and he will make sure I know it.

"Sounds wonderful," she mumbles while scanning the items on the shelves, still twirling her hair. She's adorable. I have no shame while I take my turn to check Dawn out, and I look my fill. I have never been shopping with a woman before. There are a lot of things that I have never considered doing with a woman, like saying adorable, going to brunch and taking a long walk around town, but I am enjoying it. Even food shopping doesn't feel like a chore with Dawn.

She reaches for an item that is too high for her to get. Her whole body stretches out right before my eyes. The back of her shirt rises, exposing a small strip of skin. My body moves on its own. I lay a hand on her hip to balance her and feel her smooth skin. She shivers as she comes down off her toes. Our eyes meet, and we gaze at each other while I grab the item she was trying to reach.

Taking the item, Dawn still holds my gaze. Neither of us move. My hand on her back is still on her skin. Every nerve-ending sends tingles through my body. She is letting me touch her, but I want to devour her. I don't even care that we are in the middle of the grocery store.

"Thank you," she whispers. Her eyes darken as they roam down to my lips, and for a half-second, I contemplate kissing her.

Instead, I clear my throat, send a silent prayer she doesn't notice the tent I am pitching, and mumble, "Anytime."

Several seconds go by—hell, eternity could have slipped past us—while we stare at each other. So much is being said in this moment. My free hand reaches forward tucking the small strand of hair she likes to twirl behind her ear.

Dawn shivers. Breaking our connection, she looks down at what she's holding. "Thank you," she repeats, avoiding my stare like she knows we both are close to getting swept away.

"You said that," I smile. Her cheeks burning with a blush. It is then that she realizes how close we are and steps away. My fingers slide off her skin, itching to grab a hold and not let her out of their grasp. Seeing her eyes fill with worry and maybe a touch of fear, I blurt out, "My mom used to make cookies with extra chocolate chips."

"She did?" She brightens up. A tremble is still present in her voice.

I am not playing fair, baiting Dawn with talk of my mother and baking. I have learned that she misses and loved her mother dearly and doesn't mind answering questions about her. And, when I see her pull away, I can tell her something about my mother or ask her some kind of baking question and bring her back, wiping the look of worry off her beautiful face.

"She had to make several batches. Having four boys, it was a miracle she kept us all fed," I share. Her timid smile returns so I continue, "She put extra chips in for me."

"What kind of chocolate chips did she use?" she asks, and I walk us down the aisle.

"There's more than one kind?" I ask with a sheepish grin, rubbing the back of my neck.

"Do you have her recipe?" She sounds so eager, and I don't want to disappoint her, but not long after my mother died, my father packed up her stuff and locked it away in the basement. We were not allowed to go near it without risking his wrath. After I left home, I never went back to the house. Luke owns it now.

"It might be at the old house. I can ask Luke," I offer, hoping that will suffice.

She smiles with a nod then glances down the aisle we are about to leave. "I need to grab a few more things." She stops and turns, snatching up flour, sugar, and a few bags of chocolate chips. Dumping them into our cart, still smiling, she says, "The first recipe I learned by heart was my mom's double chocolate chip cookies."

"Does she have a lot of recipes?" We start a slow stroll down the next aisle. Dawn's attention is on the shelves. I long for her attention to remain on me. I'm greedy like that.

"Yes," she answers with a sad smile. "We used to bake together on her days off."

"And now you bake on your days off?"

She bites her lip again, a sure sign, I am about to touch on something Dawn isn't wanting to open up about.

"Not recently, no—," she admits. She seems to have more to say but instead of saying it, she is still chewing on her bottom lip. Her eyes shift around the aisle.

"Why did you stop?"

"Isn't it my turn to ask a question?" Dawn says and turns her back, walking away to grab baking soda. When she faces me again, the sadness has returned. Most of the questions I have asked about her recent history, Dawn avoids. Sorrow and distress are written all over her face. It isn't hard to figure out something horrible has happened to her. The more she avoids, the more my mind wonders, conjuring up all kinds of incidents. None of them good.

"Who cooked for you after your mom died?" she asks, breaking into my train of thought. I remind myself not to scare Dawn off.

"Eric," my voice sounds flat when I answer. I haven't spoken to Eric in months, and when we talk, it's about something mundane. I find avoiding him all together is the best course of action. He holds grudges. Grudges are something I don't understand.

"He's the one who took care of Jax, while you and Luke were away?" she asks, noticing the tension.

"Yes. Glad you're paying attention," I reply, hoping she doesn't ask more about my wayward brother. Our relationship is strained at best, and I haven't the faintest idea why.

Turning down another aisle, she sees an item she needs and returns with a timid smile. "Can you cook?"

"Frozen pizzas are my specialty." I laugh when she scrunches her nose. It's cute, and I want to pull her in. "Are you a frozen pizza snob?"

"My mom and I would make our own pizza," she giggles, putting a hand on the cart next to mine. She leads us further down the aisle and I like hearing her giggle.

"Don't knock it until you've tried it," I taunt, hoping to get her to laugh more. Her laughter is rare, and a treat I am coming to crave.

"Once you've had my pizza, you will never want frozen again," she teases, stopping us before we can turn into the frozen food aisle.

"I guess you'll have to cook me dinner sometime." I flash her a smug smile, hoping she will take the bait and let me spend more time with her.

"Is this what you do with all the ladies?" she says and pokes me in the side, "Get them to cook for you?"

"I have never asked a lady to cook for me." I seize the hand that poked me, and I pull her towards me. With my other hand, I lift her chin, so she looks me in the eye. I don't want her to think there have been a lot of *other women*. She isn't just *another woman* to me.

"Except me?" she mumbles. Our closeness shocks her, but she hasn't pulled away yet, so I keep my hold on her chin, letting my thumb caress her jaw.

I see her insecurities. It's not like she is trying to hide them. They are written across her face. A protectiveness blooms in my chest cavity. It's unlike the protectiveness I have for my brothers, or even Burns. This is stronger, fiercer, and a little scary.

"Except you," I whisper.

"You are pushy, Clint," she grumbles, spreading a big playful smile across my face. She wants to downplay the intensity we both feel. For now, I'll let that slide. Let her defuse the sexual tension.

"And, you are stubborn," I return. "I'll make you a deal."

"I'm listening." She narrows those beautiful blue eyes at me. She is so close. It is hard not to lean forward and touch my lips to hers.

"On your next night off, I'll buy us dinner, but you have to make us dessert."

"There you go being pushy again." She rolls her eyes before biting her lip.

"Don't be stubborn." I rub my thumb over her lip, freeing it from her teeth. "For all I know you are a lousy cook. I could get the raw end of this deal. No pun intended."

"Your incorrigible!" she hisses, pulling from my grip. She turns her back on me before twirling back around, her hands on her hips. "Fine. I'll take you up on this deal, but on one condition."

"I'm listening," I say, happy I am getting my way.

"You have to clean up."

"Clean up?" I frown, even though I will gladly scrub pots if it means more time with Dawn. I may not be good at scrubbing those pots, but I will do it.

"Yes. Clean up. You know, wash dishes, put them away, mop the floor." Dawn's smile grows, her playful side on full display. It's so fucking sexy.

"I don't know…" I rub my hand across my beard. "Do you have any references?"

"References?" Dawn repeats trying her best to look insulted but not quite able to conceal her beautiful smile. "You doubt my skills?"

"No, no. I have no doubt you can cook." I grin at her as she takes a step closer to me. We stand toe to toe, her narrowed eyes focused on me. All trace of fear and sadness gone, replaced with confidence in herself. *How many times do I have to fight the urge to kiss the hell out of her?* "I just don't know if you can cook well."

"Oh, I can cook," she says straightening her spine. I see a fiery spirit blossoming before my eyes.

"Great." I smile down at her. "I look forward to you proving it."

"Oh, I'll prove it," she repeats matter-of-factly. "And when I do, you will be scrubbing my kitchen clean."

"You've got yourself a deal."
I have another date with Dawn.

8

- Dawn -

"No touching!" I order, pointing my wooden spoon at Clint, trying but failing to look serious.

"I'm not touching anything." Clint lifts his hands up, flashing a mischievous grin that melts my resolve. There is something in his eyes that I cannot decipher but it has the butterflies in my stomach dancing.

"You keep eating the cookie dough."

He presses his lips together to hold back a laugh. His blue eyes are normally cold like a frozen lake. He is always assessing; but now, they look warm and inviting. They draw me in, and I cannot focus. This is the reason I should not be spending so much time with him.

"You're taking too long," he mutters, stepping closer to me at the counter where I am greasing two cookie sheets. My stomach muscles tighten, and I grip the butter too tightly making a greasy mess of my fingers.

"You can't rush the process," I state, putting the butter on its dish and moving to the sink to wash my hands. I turn back towards Clint in time to see him twist towards the cabinet and dig two fingers into the cookie dough.

After we finished food shopping, Clint helped me carry everything in before taking his own groceries home and running out to get a pizza. I refused to eat frozen. I cannot remember the last time I have had this much fun. The lingering effects of the fall I took out my apartment window to escape the intruder and the worry of being found has played center stage in my thoughts lately, but Clint has managed to distract me from it all. He even managed to convince me to have dinner with him before going into work. Him being extremely tall, hot and perfectly chiseled is an added bonus, but what I see in him isn't what others see. To the world he is huge, scary and reclusive with a piercing stare that can cut steel. The more time I spend with him, the kinder he gets. It is like having my own gentle giant with a sexy smile.

"You're blushing," Clint says, breaking into my thoughts. He puts cool hands on my cheeks to bring their temperature down. His calloused hands shouldn't feel comforting, but they do and they only make me blush more.

I step away from his grip and walk over to the greased cookie sheets. This puts me a good two feet away from Clint, but the move does nothing to help my red face. Glancing sideways, I catch him taking another bite of the cookie dough.

"There won't be any cookies to bake if you keep sneaking bites," I say, my face still pink, showing no signs of cooling.

"We could just eat the dough," he shrugs, two fingers scooping up cookie dough. This time he doesn't eat it but sticks his fingers toward my mouth. "You know you want some."

"Incorrigible," I mutter with a smile and lean over, taking both his fingers into my mouth and sucking off the cookie dough. Clint's eye's darken into black orbs full of what I recognize as desire. My heart stutters in my chest, and my core tightens. Taking my time, I lick up every speck of cookie dough from his fingers. Clint's free hand pulls me closer, leaving his hand on my hip. I release his fingers.

"More?"

"What?" I blink rapidly trying to put a meaning with the word, but I am too distracted by our closeness and the ache of my own desire to inch closer. I have no idea what I am doing. Clint makes me want to lose control. It's terrifying but not in the way being found terrifies me.

"Do you want another bite?" Clint winks, squeezing my hip. My chest is pressed up against his own and I wonder if he can feel my heart pounding.

"No," I breathe, debating whether I should inch over a little, letting his hand slide to my ass. *No! Focus Dawn!* I mentally reprimand myself. Stay in control.

"Are these done?" Clint breaks into my scheming and slides a greased cookie sheet closer to him and the bowl of cookie dough.

"Yes." I nod, sliding the other sheet over.

"Now what?" he asks.

"We put them on the sheets like this." Taking the spoon, I left in the bowl, I scoop a spoonful of cookie dough and place it on the sheet. I line up a few more scoops of cookie dough. Clint's fingers make slow circle patterns on my skin. It becomes a struggle to keep my breathing even. We stay like this until I have filled the sheets with cookie dough in neat rows. Lifting a cookie sheet, I start to take it to the oven when Clint takes it from my hands and grabs the other sheet.

"I'll do it," he says.

I move around him to open the oven door.

"Don't sneak anymore," I warn, watching Clint bend over the oven. His massive arms set the sheets onto shelves effortless. Everything about Clint is sexy. Inhaling deeply, I try to clear my lust-filled head, but my body refuses to let me.

"Where's your phone?" Clint asks, shutting the oven door.

"There." I point to the flip phone at the end of the counter, standing up straighter when he steps in front of me. My face is not even an inch away from his chest. "I don't really use it much," I mumble as his arms slide around my waist.

Leaning down centimeters from my lips, he pauses.

"How old is this thing?"

His breath is hot on my cheek and smells like chocolate. Before I can go in for a sample, he pulls back with my phone in his hand, and I release the breathe from my lungs, I didn't even know I was holding.

"How long should I set the timer?" he asks.

"What?"

I blink several times at Clint who has flipped open my phone.

Get it together! I think. *Breathe!*

"How long should I set the timer?" he asks again with raised eyebrows, that puckered scar lifting slightly in a snarling smirk.

"Oh," I cough. My heart is in my throat. "It doesn't have a timer."

"This thing is ancient. I can't remember the last time I saw a flip phone."

He looks it over before digging into his pocket and pulling his smartphone out.

"What should I set the timer for?" he asks again.

"A couple of minutes," I say, taking my phone from him and placing it back onto the counter. The phone is not old. It is only a few weeks old, and its only purpose is to make calls. I don't think I can even text on it. It doesn't have data. It is one of those phones you have to add minutes too.

"What should we do while we wait?" Clint asks as he leans in toward me again. His hands brush against my waist as he sets his phone down. He smells like gasoline and chocolate. The combination makes me lightheaded.

"I don't know," I choke out, wondering if he would mind if I licked his neck just to see what he tastes like. A blush crawls up my neck and face, again. I must be as red as an apple, and my thoughts must be transparent if the amusement in Clint's stare is anything to go by.

"Why don't you get a newer phone?"

"I don't need a new one," I justify, lowering my eyes from Clint's neck to his very solid, very muscled chest. I bite my cheek, holding back the urge to put my hands on him. This is exactly why I have wanted to keep my distance. My libido is taking control of my rational mind.

"Can you text?" Clint asks, his arms still framing my waist, close, but not touching. Gripping the counter, he has me locked within the cage of his arms, but he doesn't make an attempt to touch me.

"Why?" I ask his chest.

"I want to talk to you more." He lets go of the counter and reaches up to let his fingers slide down my cheek. He gently pulls my chin up, so my gaze can meet his.

"Oh," I say softly.

His eyes drop to my mouth, and a feather light touch of his thumb to the edge of my mouth liquifies me. It is a wonder I am still standing.

"Do you work tomorrow?"

"Hmm?" I ask, confused, still lost in his stare.

"Work?" he asks again with a self-satisfied smile. "Tomorrow?"

"Oh, work!" I close my eyes and shake my foggy brain. "Yes, I work tomorrow."

"Can I come see you?"

I stare up at him for a moment. All the tingles Clint elicits thrum through my body, urging me closer to him. Telling me to give in.

"Yes," I answer. A distant voice whispers in my head.

This is not a good idea.

I'm changing the plan, I whisper back, shutting the inner voice down.

"Dawn?" Clint quietly growls my name.

His handsome face is intense as he bridges the small distance between us. I forget all about my plan because kissing Clint feels like a much better plan just now. It has been a long time since I have been kissed, and I don't want to miss this opportunity, even if it costs me.

"Clint…" I whisper.

Then, an obnoxious horn repeatedly honks. The sound comes from behind me. I frown.

"Shit!" Clint hisses, releasing me.

He leans around me, picking up his phone and shuts the timer off.

"I should pull them out," I mumble, side stepping Clint.

That distant inner voice grows louder in volume as I put space between us.

You almost kissed Clint! It repeats in my head like an accusation.

This is exactly what I have been afraid would happen.

While I check on the cookies, my desire for Clint rages a war against that inner voice that insists I listen to reason. I avoid looking at him. I know that one glance at his beautiful features will silence that voice of reason, and I'll do something I will regret.

"They need a few more minutes," I breathe out, inspecting the cookies carefully because they are safer to look at than Clint.

"They smell amazing," he says close to my ear, sending those tingles down my spine.

"Will you set the timer again?" I manage to say, fighting not to lean back against his welcoming chest. Stepping away from the oven, I pick up the bowl that still has cookie dough in it and carry it to the fridge. "I'll save these for Burns."

Finally, I dare a glance at Clint. He is watching me with narrowed eyes, and his jaw is clenched.

He says, "It's getting late."

Rubbing a hand down his face and resting it on his bearded chin, he adds, "I should go so you can get ready for work."

"Ok." I nod, knowing he is right. My body is screaming, *No!*

The touching and almost kissing aren't smart for either of us, that inner voice reassures.

"I'll see you tomorrow," he says, tucking his phone in his pocket, and giving me one last look of disappointment. "You can give me those cookies you owe me then."

I drop my eyes to the ground, saying "Sure," and he leaves.

It was the smart thing to do, letting him leave before things went too far.

Protect Forever

Staring at the door Clint just left through, I rub my chest, wishing my heart would stop telling me I am lying to myself.

9

- Clint -

"Clint come have some of Dawn's cookies," Burns hollers from the bar with a half-eaten cookie in his mouth. Dawn is standing on the other side of the bar. She looks nervous. Her smile is timid.

After leaving her place last night, I tossed and turned unable to shake the image of regret on Dawn's face when I almost kissed her. All the signs were there! She wanted me to kiss her. Hell, she looked ready to pounce a couple times. Then she snapped, and with a blink of an eye, her walls went up.

"I brought some for you." She pulls out a container and slides it over. "Beer?"

"Sure." I take the seat next to Burns. Benny walks out from the kitchen carrying two plates piled with fries and his famous burgers.

"Nice to see you, Clint," he mutters barely offering a glance.

"Benny," I tip my chin up in a nod as he passes. The man never was much for words. He never treated me like I was a recluse but also never tried to chat me up with small talk. It is why I like coming here, when it isn't crowded. I wonder how he feels about Luke coming back into town.

"How's the shop?" Burns asks nonchalantly as Dawn brings over a beer.

"Busy. I'll be hiring some part-time help soon," I grunt, taking a drink and watching Dawn wring her fingers. "These are delicious." I hold up one of her cookies.

Relaxing, she brightens, beaming a beautiful smile my way. My chest expands with pride and maybe a little hope.

"Miss Janet can bake too." Burns sighs over another cookie.

I give him a side glance. The old man looks utterly smitten. "How'd brunch go?" I wink at Dawn with a knowing smile.

"She agreed to be my date to the Fall Festival," Burns grins, wiggling his eyebrows.

"Good job, old man," I pat his shoulder, looking at Dawn. "Maybe you can give me some pointers. I can't get Dawn to agree to go with me."

"I didn't say I wouldn't go," she protests with a deep blush. I love that blush. "I said I might have to work."

"So, you *will* ask for it off?" I raise an eyebrow.

"Maybe," she rolls her eyes.

I'll take a maybe. It's better than the rejection she's prone to.

"What are you worried about?" Burns asks Dawn, munching on another cookie. "Benny won't mind you taking it off. You can come check out Miss Janet's cherry pie."

"See," I smile wide, "Burns agrees."

"I'm still new. I have got to put my time in before I start asking for it off," she objects.

"Benny may want to take off to be with his family."

"Dawn," Benny cuts in, coming around the bar, "The softball games have just ended. It's about to get busy."

"Benny, can you give Dawn here next Saturday off?" Burns interrupts.

Sneaky devil!

I will never complain when he pokes his nose where it doesn't belong if he can coax Dawn into going to the Fall Festival with me.

Dawn frowns with a glare at Burns before turning to give Benny her full attention. "I'll pull a couple of cases from the fridge. The chest is getting low."

"I'll handle that," Benny says, shifting narrowed eyes from Dawn to Burns and I. "Can you pull out more coasters and napkins from the back?"

"Sure." She turns and leaves us.

I watch her leave, enjoying her backside, only mildly disappointed she didn't try to get the day off. There is still a chance Burns can work his magic on Benny and Dawn.

"Now, you two better not be harassing my bartender," Benny warns with a pointed stare at Burns.

"Me?" Burns innocently asks, pointing to himself, "Never, but this guy?" He points his thumb at me and snorts, "You need to be careful of."

"Just don't get in the way of her doing her job," Benny rolls his eyes and leaves us.

"Excuse me, Burns," I stand without a glance his way and head for the back-storage closet Dawn disappeared into. If it is going to get crowded, I rather head out and meet her back here at closing. Plus, it looks like I may need to do a little begging.

Nudging the partially opened door further in, I see that Dawn is piling packages of napkins from an open box onto a shelf. Her skinny jeans sculpt her ass like a masterpiece. Roaming my eyes up her backside, to her exposed neck, my fingers itch to trace the same path.

"Sweetness," I murmur close to her ear.

Dropping the napkins, a gasp escapes her lips as she spins around so fast she pushes herself back into the shelf.

"Whoa." I say. I put my hands out, attempting to catch her, but I am unsure if I should touch her. Deep breaths make her chest heave rapidly. My insides wrench when I see her eyes are full of panic. The fear there guts me.

"It's ok… It's ok… It's ok," I repeat until her breathing evens out, and I think it is ok to touch her. I wrap one arm around her waist and snake the other up her back, fisting her hair in my fingers and pulling her into my chest. "It's ok," I whisper again.

"I'm sorry," she mumbles into my chest. Her hands are on my abs, making my dick twitch. *It can be a bastard sometimes.*

"What are you sorry for?" I ask as I pull her slightly away from my chest so I can see her face. She is looking at my chest. Fear lingers in those bewitching blue eyes. They look haunted.

"I get scared easily," she admits.

"I can see that." I narrow my eyes and pull her in closer. I want to ask why but think better of it. She is letting me hold her and not running. I am making progress. I don't want those walls of hers going up right now. Not when she needs something to sooth her fear away.

"I should get back to work," she says hesitantly but doesn't pull away. Giving her a quick squeeze, I lightly kiss the top of her head—I doubt she even notices—and breathe in her sugary scent.

"Sweetness," I whisper into her ear, "I'm going to take off. I'll be back at closing."

She tips her chin up so our eyes meet, and I see relief. It is the perfect moment to lean down and kiss her, but I don't, not in a storage closet in a bar. It doesn't feel right, so I fight my body and let go of her.

"Is Burns staying?" she asks while I help her gather up the packages of coasters and napkins.

"I'm going to try and get him to go home, but the man is stubborn with a soft spot for you," I say with a wink down at her over an arm load of coasters.

"You got the lazy yuppy to work?" Burns jokes as we emerge from the back.

"Always telling lies," I return, dropping the coasters onto the edge of the bar.

"Clint, you ready to blow this joint?" Burns asks, holding his cell phone at arm's length and trying to read whatever is on the screen.

"Even he has a newer cell phone," I point out with a teasing smile.

Rolling her eyes, Dawn opens a package of napkins her hands shaking. She is still tense. Her slow recovery bothers me. It is uncommon for someone to react the way she did. This is the third time I have seen her freak out like this. The more I think on it, the more my gut twists into a knot.

"Yo!" Burns snaps his fingers in my face. "Earth to Clint."

"What?" I growl.

"Give me a ride to Miss Janet's?" he winks. "Her bunco party just ended."

"Cindy know you're out?" I ask and look over at the old man, noticing for the first time how nicely he is dressed. Even his thinning white hair is combed.

"I told her not to wait up," Burns snaps. "Not that it's any of *your* business."

"All right, old man," I sigh, not wanting to push him. At least he's not going to be out late drinking.

"Sweetness! We're leaving."

Burns waves at Dawn, sliding off the stool and heading for the door. There is an extra swing in his step that curves my lips up. I don't even care that he keeps calling Dawn 'Sweetness.' It is nice seeing the old man look young again.

I walk back over to Dawn. Her eyes are wide with uncertainty. I am about to draw my fingers across her cheek when Benny walks out of the kitchen, hauling two cases of beer.

"You two leaving?" he asks, putting the cases down.

"Yeah," I say disappointed, pulling my wallet out. I hand over some cash to Dawn and whisper, "I'll be back."

Nodding, she takes the cash and starts counting out change.

"Keep it."

"Thank you," she whispers with a sad smile. I hate that sadness. I want nothing more than to take it away.

I watch her for a couple of seconds as something foreign and possessive takes root in me. I know nothing will ever be the same.

10

- Dawn -

"Ah, good. Clint, can you take Dawn home?" Benny asks as he and I walk out of the bar for the night. Seeing Clint waiting by the door is more than a pleasant sight. It causes all kinds of butterflies to swarm in my stomach, spiking my heart rate and putting a blush on my face. Pushing off the wall where he is leaning, he winks at me with his cocky grin, like he can read my thoughts.

"Of course," Clint says, and I am still staring.

Last night, I listened to the voice in my head telling me not to deviate from my plan, but earlier when Clint wrapped me up in his arms, soothing my fear, I silenced the nagging and embraced the possibilities. All evening, I have wondered what he could possibly see in me. I am a shell of a person, a ghost. Yet, his blue eyes seem to see something in me. Maybe, I am not as hollow as I thought.

"See you tomorrow," Benny calls out, waving as he climbs into his truck leaving me alone with Clint. I don't know why I am so nervous. I wasn't nearly this nervous when he picked me up for Brunch. Something has shifted between us, and by the way Clint is eyeing me, he feels it too.

Clint takes a step towards me, and a shiver slithers down my spine, not from the cold but from the energy that he sparks. Tucking my arms tightly around myself, I turn from him and head towards my house. I need to burn off some of this nervous energy, but Clint gently pulls me back towards him. Pulling his coat off, he wraps it around me. The combination of grease and gasoline invades my nostrils making me dizzy. I snake my arms through the oversized sleeves. Who knew something like gasoline could smell so good? A feather light touch from Clint pushes my chin up forcing me to look at him. There is a protectiveness there that warms me to my core.

"Ready?" he asks, searching my face. He softly pushes my hair behind my ear. His fingers are gentle as they slide down my arm, taking my hand. Familiar tingles shoot through my veins, causing my heart to skip a beat. I cannot pull away even if I wanted to. If anything, I am finding myself wanting to draw closer to him. "You need to wear a warmer coat," he says.

"Hm?" I ask, still reeling over the intimacy I cannot deny between him and I. The way his thumb draws circles on my skin sends more tingles throughout my body, heating up places I thought long dead.

"You need to wear a warmer coat," he repeats with a chuckle, his voice like the purr of a lion, gentle, yet commanding.

"Oh," I say, scrunching my nose. "I don't have one. Just my jean jacket."

"I guess you'll have to hold on to mine," Clint replies, peering down at me with his gentle smile. It is one of those contagious smiles that you cannot stop yourself from returning, but it is one he only lets me and maybe Burns see. I have a feeling that he does not let the rest of the world see this soft side of him.

The idea of keeping Clint's coat excites me more than it should, and I cannot help blurting out, "Benny is letting me off for the Fall Festival." I inhale another wave of the jacket's intoxicating smell, letting it sooth me. *Why am I always so awkward around him?*

Clint squeezes my hand with one hand while his free hand caresses my face from my cheek down to my jaw before he lifts my chin forcing me to look at him.

"Let me take you to the Fall Festival," he whispers, sending more tingles down my spine. It is not a question, but a demand.

Unable to stop myself, I lean into him. His hand wraps around my neck. His other hand releases mine before tugging at my waist.

"Say *yes*," he orders, our lips inching closer.

All I can do is nod. The second his lips touch mine, I lose my restraint and all control. He is slow and tentative, only taking what I am willing to give him. I want to give him more.

He cocoons me within his arms. He pulls me in tighter, crushing me to his chest like it is a struggle for him to stay patient. It has been so long since anyone has touched me. My fried nerve endings are sparking to life and not from fear, but from desire. Unable to hold back, I deepen the kiss, and Clint responds, devouring my mouth with a growl.

God, he tastes good. Like beer and something smokey with a hint of chocolate from my cookies.

He is nothing like I expected. He is soft where I thought he would be hard. His tongue is desperate to taste me. I thought he would be demanding, but his mouth only gives. If this is how it will feel to kiss Clint, I will gladly make it my full-time job, safely wrapped up in his deliciousness. This kiss is the kind of kiss that touches your mind, body, and soul. It is a kiss that wakes sleeping princesses and breaks curses. I could go my whole life never to kiss again if the memory of this kiss stays fresh in my mind.

Clint pulls back, I blink a couple times before I can collect myself. Both of us pant as he rests his forehead against mine. I wonder if he felt it too, but neither of us speaks. I can barely believe this is real. I fear it will all disappear, and I'll be back in my nightmare of loneliness and despair.

"I should get you home." Clint finally breaks the silence. It is too dark to read his face, but I swear he is struggling to pull himself away from me. My hands are still fisted in his shirt when he steps away. I don't want to let go. Taking one of my hands in his, he pulls me to his side. His thumb draws circles against my skin again. I let the tingles wash over me while we walk in silence to my house.

Climbing my porch steps, he does not follow. Letting go of his hand, I turn and face him at eye level. The porch light is dim, casting a yellow light over us. His eyes study me as I bite my lip, debating on whether I should invite him in. I know he is waiting for me to make the first move, but I lost the ability to be brave long ago. I need him to push me.

"Are you off before the Fall Festival?" he asks. His thumb pulls my lip gently from my teeth.

"Wednesday." I shiver when his thumb gently runs over my bottom lip.

"Can I take you out again?" he asks, watching my mouth.

"Yes." I grin.

His hand moves to cup my head, and I lean into it. His other hand wraps around my neck tilting my head towards him as he searches my face. The fierce look he gives me is primal and possessive, he looks ready to pounce.

"Go inside and lock the door. I'll see you tomorrow," he growls, his breath warm against my face, and he kisses me one more time. I can feel his tense muscles restraining him, and all too soon, he lets me go.

I have definitely altered my course, and something deep and quiet tells me this path might be the most dangerous one I follow.

*****

"Is that sugar?" I ask when Clint holds out a five-pound bag of sugar. It looks tiny in his hand.

"Sweetness," he greets me from my door. Stepping inside, he lifts my chin with his free hand, before saying, "Flowers are boring."

I don't have time to respond as his mouth descends onto mine. Tingles ignite, burning up the nervousness I was feeling leading up to our first official date. Clint smells fresh and minty with a hint of gasoline. I am coming to love his smell. It is comforting, and soothing.

Gently his lips taste mine, picking up speed as I demand more of him. Without breaking our connection, Clint moves us further into the house, shutting the door before turning us both and backing me up against it. I press into him, completely forgetting everything. My mind is consumed with Clint and the way he feels. My body burns, humming to life as Clint presses against me. I can feel all of him. A moan escapes my lips, and Clint stiffens before pushing away. I did not mean it as a protest. It just came out as my befuddled mind began to awaken.

"Sorry Sweetness, but if I don't stop now, I'll likely embarrass myself," He chuckles as he slides a strand of my hair behind my ear.

Blinking up at him, a deep blush spreads over my entire body. Losing control like that was not on my agenda. Not at all part of my plan. *What is he doing to me?*

"I should put this away," I breath out, taking the sugar from his hand and putting it on the kitchen counter.

"Do you like steak?" Clint asks, not moving away from the door, definitely a good thing because I still don't quite trust myself in close proximity to him. God, he looks amazing in loose fitting jeans and a V-neck shirt. It is different from the clothes he normally wears. I have grown fond of his Colson Auto Body shirts, but I like his clean-shaven look too.

"Dawn?" Clint calls me back to awareness.

"What?" I ask, realizing that I am staring. *Can I just stop?*

"Steak?" Clint asks with a smug grin, his hands shoved into his jeans. He holds back a laugh. He must think that I am a complete spaz.

"Sure." I squeak with a nervous tremble. *How am I going to get through this date?*

All day, when I wasn't thinking about how utterly foolish I am being, I daydreamed about what this date was going to be like. None of my scenarios included me making a spectacle out of myself.

"Come on," Clint beckons, pulling his hand out of his pocket for me to take, "There is a great steak house in River Bend, the town over."

I take Clint's hand, and he waits while I lock up my house. He doesn't release my hand until he has led me to his truck. Opening the passenger door, he helps me in, his fingers brushing softly against my lower back. Tingles make me wobbly on my feet while I attempt to look graceful climbing up into the cab. Clint flashes me a smug grin before shutting the door and jogging over to the driver's side. I try to take a few calming breathes but nothing seems to want to calm the buildup of desire Clint sparks inside of me.

The trip to River Bend is quiet, not the uncomfortable quiet of a first date, a peaceful quiet, something Clint and I have mastered. He turns the radio on to some slow country, and I let the music sooth my nerves some. I am being ridiculous but cannot help feeling so out of my league with him. Clint is unlike any man I have ever known, gentle yet intimidating, kind and patient, extremely sexy, persistent and a little pushy. He makes it too easy to forget why I am here and that I have no idea what tomorrow will bring.

"Stay there," Clint says after putting his truck in park and killing the engine.

Pausing after undoing my seatbelt, I look over at him, but he is already climbing out of the truck. I watch him as he walks around the hood to my side. Opening the door, he holds out a hand for me. Sucking a breath, I grab it. The tingles cascade through my body. No one has ever opened my car door for me. Not that I have had a lot of experience with dating, but still the gesture causes my heart to skip. I like it. It makes me feel special, and I am starting to like feeling special. Only, I shouldn't, and hasn't that always been the problem?

"What's that look for?" Clint asks taking my hand in his, his other hand on my hip. Every place he touches warms my skin and makes it difficult not to want to lean in more closely and take in his intoxicating scent.

"What look?" I ask as I peer at him, trying not to tumble out of his truck. The truck is the perfect size for Clint. He is a giant, but I look like I am trying to climb out of a monster truck, and there is no attractive way to do that.

"You look ready to run," Clint says. He frowns, pulling me close, making no attempt to move.

"I don't want to run," I deny. I wish he could not read me so well.

Clint looks ready to say something but does not. Instead, he pulls me away from the truck, shutting and locking the door before leading me toward River Bend Steakhouse.

It isn't terribly busy, and we are seated quickly at a table by a window. I love the atmosphere, with its sports team uniforms framed next to team pictures. Most of the uniforms and pictures are from the local college. Clint tells me that a few uniforms and pictures are from River Bend High School and some from the Peak Valley High baseball team, that won state a few years back, are displayed not far from where we sit.

"Good evening. I'll be your server for the night. I'm Alex," a young man announces before launching into the drink specials. I have never been much of a drinker and order water. Clint orders a beer.

"You sure you don't want something other than water? Wine?" Clint asks after Alex walks away to put our drink order in.

"I know nothing about wine. I wouldn't know where to begin," I admit, embarrassment coloring my cheeks. This is yet another reminder that I'm in over my head when it comes to dating. After high school, I only dated one man and his idea of a date was going to a motorcycle bar and playing darts or pool.

"I can ask the server to pick something for you," Clint offers before pressing his lips together, piercing me with his sexy yet terrifying stare.

"You intend to spoil me, don't you?" I blurt out, not meaning to say it out loud. I cover my mouth before releasing a giggle.

"Yes, and you don't make it easy." Clint smiles back. Reaching over, he grabs my hand and entwines our fingers. "Maybe you can let your guard down for the night."

"It's safer if I keep it up," I admit, immediately regretting the words that have left my mouth. *What is wrong with me? I haven't even had a drink yet.* Clint makes it so easy to share what I'm thinking, only what I'm thinking usually makes him want to ask more questions, questions I don't want to answer.

"Safer how?" Clint asks, his eyes narrowing, and his hand tightening around mine.

"How about you ask the server to pair some wine with my food?" I suggest, aiming to change the subject. For the second time tonight, Clint looks ready to say something but doesn't, much to my relief.

"What do you plan to order?" he asks, releasing my hand to open his menu.

"I don't know. What is good here?" I ask, opening my own menu, feeling the loss of his hand deep in my chest.

"Their steak," Clint grunts still not looking at me. "You should try their filet mignon."

"Really?" I ask, watching him over my menu. "I have never had it."

"Then get it. Trust me, you'll like it."

"How do you know I'll like it?" I tease, hoping to get him to look at me again. I don't like ruining all our moments with my inability to keep my mouth shut, but I feel it is necessary not to share too much even if it feels like I am lying.

"I don't, but I want to know everything about you," Clint answers seriously. I was not expecting that, but I should have been. Clint has been nothing but honest with me. I'm the one keeping secrets and holding him at arm's length.

Silence falls over us while we both look over the menu. It is a welcome relief when Alex returns with our drinks. "Have you both decided what you'd like to order?"

"Yes," Clint says as I nod in agreement.

"And what would you like Miss?" Alex turns to me, pulling his notepad and pen out.

133

"I'll try the filet mignon with the garlic mashed potatoes and a side salad with honey mustard dressing." I say, glancing at Clint. A ghost of a smile appears on his face that relaxes some of the tension in my shoulders.

"How would you like that cooked?" Alex asks me. I look at him mystified. *Cooked? Preferably on a grill?*

"She'll like it medium well," Clint answers for me much to my relief. "Also, can you bring her a glass of wine that will pair well with it?"

"Of course, we have a great house red that pairs nicely." Alex smiles turning his attention to Clint. "And you sir?"

"Ribeye, medium rare with garlic mashed potatoes and a side salad with ranch dressing."

Clint takes my menu and hands it to Alex, along with his own.

"I'll get these orders in for you." Alex says, taking the menus before walking away.

"For someone who likes to brag about her cooking abilities, I find it hard to believe you've never had steak," Clint says with a small smile.

"It's too expensive. And, I don't brag!" I protest, unable to hold back my smile. "Besides, you liked my cookies."

"I did like your cookies," He says, shrugging before taking a drink from his beer. "But, I can't say for sure that you are good cook."

"Excuse me?" I blink in horror, recalling his greedy consumption of cookie dough the other night.

"I still require more proof." He winks at me with a smile that melts my insides and heats my core. *Where is my self-control? That's right I have none.*

"You're just as bad as Burns." I roll my eyes taking a sip from my water, hoping it will cool me down.

"Whoa, there's no need for name calling, Sweetness," he laughs. I love his laugh, its deep tone, the way it rumbles from his chest, and how genuine it is. Clint is stoic by nature, but when he shows his tender side, I find him irresistible.

"Incorrigible!" I mutter, trying my hardest not to laugh. He can be so damn sexy when he breaks out his sense of humor. A small part of me wants to be the only one who gets to see this side of Clint, and that small part is growing.

"I'm just saying that I need to sample some more of your cooking before I can truly weigh in on your talents," he says with laughter in his eyes. When he smiles, his eyes remind me of clear blue ocean water, unlike the icy blue I am used to seeing.

"You're just saying that so you can spend more time with me." I narrow my eyes at him, but I know I will be cooking up a storm for him. "I'm on to your baiting Clint."

"Absolutely, I am baiting you," Clint agrees, nodding his head, "Without shame."

I am in so much trouble.

11

- Clint -

"Would you like another glass of wine?" Alex, our server, asks out of nowhere. I have been so caught up with Dawn, I seemed to have forgotten where we are. Not that it is hard to do when you have the most beautiful woman sitting across from you.

"I shouldn't," she sighs into her almost empty wine glass. I was able to coax her into another glass after our meal and a third with dessert. Her cheeks are slightly pink, and her guard is down. Call me a bastard for letting her get a little tipsy, but I want her to know she can relax around me, and I want to know why she builds those damn walls. Slowly, and maybe I am being a little sneaky, I am tearing them down.

Dawn's early comment about opening up not being safe isn't lost on me. It is driving me nuts knowing she doesn't feel safe. I am not a fool. I know there is someone responsible for her fear. Women do not shut themselves off from the world unless something horrible has happened to them, and the idea of something happening to Dawn, damn near kills me. I wish…, no I need, for her to let me in so I can promise to protect her from whoever has her so damn scared.

"We'll take the check," I tell Alex who already has it ready and slides it to me.

"Can I help pay?" Dawn asks with a shy smile after Alex walks away.

"No," I grunt, resisting the urge to roll my eyes as I pull out my wallet. If I had my way, I'd never let her pay. Call me old fashion, but I don't think Dawn has ever been pampered, and I would like…, no I need, to do so.

"I drank a lot of wine. At least let me pay the tip." She tries again, laying her hand on my forearm. Her touch sends tingles through my arm, and I cannot help but fantasize about her touching me more. When she touches me, I cannot focus, and my mind drifts to much more tantalizing thoughts.

"No." I shake my head. I want to believe our feelings are mutual, but I need to maintain a slow pace with her.

Damn she is making it hard. I need to continue to be patient and hope like hell she finally lets me in.

"Stubborn," she mutters, lifting her hand and crossing her arms across her chest. It pushes her breasts up, revealing more cleavage and sending signals to my dick that are not so patient. God, she is beautiful, even when she is frowning at me.

"Ready?" I ask, after leaving some cash. Standing up, I offer her my hand. She takes it as she stands up from her chair. I pull her into my side. Her heavenly scent drifts toward me. I want…, no I need, her scent all over me.

Seeing that she is looking up at me, I lean down briefly to kiss her lips, tasting a hint of wine and chocolate cake. I pull away leaving her wanting more. Her eyes close as she melts further into my side. I want…, no I need, more but do not trust myself to stop if given the chance.

"You smell good," she mumbles, opening her eyes.

"So, do you, Sweetness," I say, grinning down at her before leading her out of the restaurant and to my truck. She is safely tucked into my side, where she belongs. *She just doesn't know it yet.*

I lift her into her seat and help fasten her seatbelt, ignoring her complaints that she can handle it while calling me stubborn. I sneak one more quick kiss before slamming the door and jogging around to the driver's side. She watches me with her head resting against the head rest, turned toward me, smiling that sweet smile. Those bewitching eyes are like a sucker punch to my gut. I get lost in them, picturing a future I never thought was available for someone like me.

I turn on the radio. We sit in comfortable silence as I make my way to the highway that will lead us back to Peak Valley. The night is cool as the fall season approaches. There is not a cloud in sight. The full moon shines a soft silver light across Dawn's face, and I fight the urge to stare at her instead of the road.

"You're very handsome, yet scary," she whispers. Her head is still resting against the head rest. Her gaze never leaves me.

"Are you scared of me?" I ask, sucking a breath in. My heart beats a little faster. I have tried hard not to be another source of fear for Dawn. I can handle others fearing me, even my town fearing me, but I cannot handle the thought of Dawn fearing me.

"No," she sighs much to my relief, and closes her eyes. I rest my hand over hers. She flips her hand and entwines our fingers before drifting to sleep. Her hand is silky smooth against my calloused hand, but they fit perfectly together, as if it were fate. I never really believed in fate but I'm starting to now.

My phone buzzes in my pocket half a dozen times on the way home but I don't dare let go of Dawn's hand. I let her sleep until I pull into her driveway and even then, it tests my will to wake her. She looks peaceful in her sleep, relaxed, as if she doesn't have a care in the world. I could sit here all night and watch her sleep, but another buzz from my phone reminds me that someone is trying hard to get my attention.

Reluctantly letting go of Dawn's hand, I fish my phone from my pocket only to see several missed calls from Luke along with a few text messages. Putting my phone back in my pocket, thinking that I'll call him later, I climb out of my truck.

When I open the passenger door, Dawn stirs a little but does not wake up. I am tempted to carry her in and put her to bed, but I don't think I could resist climbing in with her. Besides, I am not keen on going through her purse to find her keys. Girls hate that shit, right?

"Dawn," I whisper close to her ear before kissing her temple. "You're home."

"Hmm." She stretches before opening her bewitching blue eyes that simply take my breath away. "I slept the whole way?" she asks.

"Yep," I answer, reaching across her lap to unfasten her seatbelt.

"Sorry," she mumbles sounding groggy as she reaches for her purse. I snatch it up for her before lifting her from her seat. Her arms instantly wrap around my shoulders pulling her soft body against mine. Slowly, I let her slide down until her feet hit the ground, but I don't let her go. I feel every inch of her and want nothing more than to push her against my truck and make her moan like she did when I picked her up. Only, she has been drinking and is not quite ready for that. So, I use the last of my restraint kissing her softly before pulling away.

I allow only my hand to take hers, and I walk her to her porch. She begins to walk up the stairs, and I let go.

"Would you like to come..." she starts to ask before a big yawn cuts off her words.

"Go inside, lock your door and get some sleep," I tell her and nod toward her front door. "I'll see you tomorrow."

Dawn yawns again, nodding her head before unlocking her door. She waves as she shuts the door, and I wait until I hear the locks click into place before heading back to my truck. I regret not kissing her, but I know I wouldn't have been able to stop.

On my way home, my phone buzzes again. This time I answer, hearing Luke's angry voice demanding to know where I am at.

"I'm almost home," I snap, annoyed. "I'm two minutes away."

"I'm waiting," he grunts, sounding equally annoyed before hanging up on me.

When I arrive, Luke is sitting on his tailgate looking wrecked with a bottle of whiskey in one hand and his other hand bandaged up in gauze. I pull into my parking spot beside my shop next to a set of stairs that lead to my apartment. Luke is at my door before I can climb out of the truck.

"Where've you been?" he asks, his words slurring together.

"Out," I grumble before nodding to his hand. "What happened there?"

"Accident," he grunts following me up my stairs. Apparently, he plans to leave out the details. "You remember Roy Cantana?"

"Yeah. He brings his BMW in every three months like clockwork," I say as I flip my apartment lights on.

I remodeled the place a few years ago, turning it into an open-concept floorplan and an awesome bachelor pad. *I wonder what Dawn will think of it.*

"Why?" I ask.

"He's a doctor at the hospital," Luke growls taking a shot of whiskey on his way to my sofa.

Crashing into the cushions, he raises his bandaged hand. "Stitched my hand up."

"Should you be drinking?" I ask, throwing my keys onto the island that I use as a dinner table, walking to the fridge, pulling a cold beer out and twisting the top.

"I'm not on any pain meds. Needed something stronger," Luke says, now holding up his bottle of whiskey. "He's Amber's boss."

"Ahh, yeah Roy's a doctor at the hospital she works at." I come over and sit at the other end of my sofa. I snatch up the remote and turn the TV on. "I didn't know he was Amber's boss."

"Maybe he's not," Luke says. He shrugs, his focus on the TV. "Do you remember him from high school?"

"No," I say, stopping on Sports Center. "Wasn't he a couple years ahead of you?"

"Yeah, total douche bag."

"Why do you say that?" I ask, and immediately regret it because Luke turns and glares at me. "He seems cool," I add.

"The entire time he was stitching my hand, he was flirting with Amber," Luke growls, taking a shot, wiping his mouth with his bandaged hand before spitting. "It was completely inappropriate."

"Hmm." I bite back the urge to laugh. Pissing off an already pissed off Luke equals guy drama I would rather not partake in. Besides, I like Roy. He knows cars, and I like having his business. Isn't he married?

143

"You should have heard the way he was talking to her," Luke goes on. "It wasn't professional. Isn't there a rule against that kind of thing?"

"Hmm."

It's pointless to say anything when Luke is on a rant. Disagreeing with him only angers him more and agreeing with him riles him up more. Especially when Amber is involved. It is better to stay neutral and let him blow off some steam.

"I think I'll lodge a complaint," Luke grumbles and takes another shot of whiskey.

I think that I should take the bottle from him, but the only way to do that is to wrestle it from him, and I am not in the mood.

"What do you think?" Luke asks.

"Hmm." I grunt, quickly chugging from my beer, so I don't have to answer.

"Amber said I was overreacting," Luke continues, "but I think she's worried about losing her job."

"Don't make things difficult for her." I finally chime in with a warning look. "She's got two kids to care for."

"I can't do nothing!" Luke cries out finally putting the whiskey bottle down on my coffee table. "Besides, I can help her. It's better than her working for that sleaze bag."

"She doesn't want your help." I say, breaking my rule not to engage, but Luke needs to leave Amber alone or he's going to lose her for good.

"Like Dawn doesn't want your help," Luke spits out, and now I'm officially pissed. He can come over and bitch all he wants, but he needs to leave Dawn out of it.

"Low blow," I say, standing up before draining my beer. I know he is drunk, but his words strike a chord. It is different with Dawn. "Don't fuck with Amber's life Luke. You did that once and it ended badly. Do it again, and she'll never forgive you."

Luke mutters something under his breath before kicking his boots off and laying down on my sofa before he hollers, "Wake me before you head down to work."

"She'll come around Luke," I say over my shoulder as I head for my bedroom knowing I'm speaking to myself too. "Just be patient."

12

- Dawn -

"I still don't understand why kissing Clint is a bad thing," Amber says, combing through her stuffed, over-flowing closet. Having packed only the necessities, my wardrobe is seriously lacking in any dateable clothes and I needed help. Amber having way too many clothes (she does not like to give anything away) offered to let me borrow something.

"Because I like it too much," I huff as I fall back onto her bed. It took three tries before I finally built up enough courage to come over. Once she opened her door, her friendly smile led me to spill my guts. It was like a dam broke and all the things I have wanted to share with Sarah but couldn't risk calling her came flooding out.

"I know that feeling," she mutters from her closet. I wonder what she and Luke have been up too. "Did I tell you that Luke showed up at the hospital last night?"

"No. What happened?" I ask, eyeing her curiously as she pulls herself from her closet.

"He had a hand laceration that needed stitches." She tells me while pulling shoes from her closet. "He refused to let anyone but me help him, walked through the ER looking for me like it was his right."

"Are you serious?"

"He's such an arrogant, ugh!" She cries out snatching an empty shoe box and tossing it toward her trash basket. "The man seriously knows how to get under my skin."

"So, what happened?" I coax, wanting more details because when it comes to Luke and Amber you know it will be juicy.

"To explain will require wine," Amber sighs standing, "Want some?"

"Small glass please."

Amber disappears for a few minutes while I look through the clothes, she wants to get rid of. *Geez she has a lot of clothes!* I want them all. Her wardrobe is full of flowery dresses and bohemian blouses. It's a unique style that Amber can pull off with her cat eyes and flirty smile but I'm not so sure I can. My style has always been jeans and a v-neck shirt. I always went for something practical and comfortable, but maybe being a little daring with the wardrobe can't hurt.

"Luke has this uncanny ability to find me no matter how hard I try to hide from him," Amber says once she enters her bedroom, handing me my glass of wine. "Walks into the room where I'm taking a patient's blood pressure and sticks his bloody hand in my face and asks me to fix it, like I'm his mother or something."

"I don't think he sees you as anything remotely related to his mother," I giggle sitting my wine down to lift up a dress against my body.

"Whose side are you on?" she asks, narrowing her eyes at me.

"Yours." I swallow a laugh that tries to escape, while trying to hold a straight face. "Definitely yours."

"Good." She winks, sipping her wine where she sits in front of her closet surrounded by piles of clothes. "Well, I get him into a room and clean up his laceration before calling for the ER doctor to come stitch him up. Only when Dr. Cantana comes in, Luke turns it into a pissing contest with him. I swear there was so much testosterone being thrown around I thought I was going to have to call security."

"Luke was going to fight the doctor?" I ask in disbelief. Luke is very protective of Amber, but I didn't really think he would pick a fight. Not that I know him very well, but he seems a lot like Clint who is not one to start a fight..., finish a fight yes, but not instigate one.

"I doubt it would have turned into a fight," she breathes out. "Luke isn't like that, but he cornered me afterwards demanding to know what was going on between me and Dr. Cantana."

"Is something going on?" I ask with a smirk.

"No!" She grabs a dress and throws it at me. "He's happily married with a kid on the way."

"Oh. So, what did Luke say to that?"

"Nothing. I didn't tell him." Amber looks away trying to look nonchalant, but I think she feels a little guilty about it.

"Why not?"

"I don't know!" she huffs before taking a large sip of wine. "Because it's none of his business!"

"I bet he wasn't happy."

"No. He wasn't," Amber says, looking remorseful as she bites her lip.

"Are all the Colson boys, so—"

"Intense?" Amber finishes for me. "Yes, but Clint is by far the most intense. Does the man ever smile?"

"He smiles, and he's gentle," I say laying back onto Amber's bed thinking about the dinner we had last night.

"Sounds like you are falling for him," Amber observes pulling several outfits out of her closet. "I think these will fit you nicely."

"Wait go back." I sit up on her bed. "I'm not falling for Clint."

"Oh, *Sweetness*, you most definitely are," Amber says, mockingly. She lays the clothes down on the bed before taking a seat next to me. "The look on your face is evidence enough."

"I'm not falling for Clint," I repeat more to myself. "It's just the newness of a relationship."

"Is it such a bad thing?" Amber asks, bunching her eyebrows together, "Falling for Clint?"

"Yes!" I cry out, covering my face. This cannot be happening. But the inner voice I like to ignore agrees with Amber, *I am falling for Clint.*

"Is it because we lied about you being a Baker?" Amber asks.

"That, and I really don't know what my future holds," I sigh, rubbing my temples. "It was never part of my plan."

"Your plan?" Amber scrunches her face in confusion. "Do you plan to go back to Charleston?"

"No. I'll never go back there."

Even if Sarah pulls off a miracle, I cannot return. There are too many bad memories and too few good ones.

"I'm confused?" Amber stands looking down at me, and I wonder if I should let her know everything. Sarah only told them I needed to get away and live off the grid. No one but Sarah knows the fully scary story. Amber is Sarah's sister, and even though I cannot explain how, I just know I can trust her. It must be a Baker trait.

"I can see myself having a future here," I shrug, hoping I sound reassuring, "but you never know."

"Dawn," Amber says, putting her hands on her hips and giving me her mom stare, "Life will never have any guarantees, but if you don't take chances you never will experience anything worth experiencing."

"Like kissing Clint?" I ask with a smirk.

"Like kissing Clint," she repeats with a wink. She holds up a teal chiffon and grey maxi dress and asks, "How about this?"

Standing up, I take the dress and hold it against my body. "Too long?"

"Maybe a little. Keep it out though." Amber dives back into her closet. "Have you talked to Sarah about Clint?" Her voice is muffled in the closet.

"No. I'll try and call her tonight." I admit as Emily, Amber's daughter, skips into the room with a big toothless smile and a dripping popsicle. Her brown hair and green eyes make her the spitting image of her mother. "I imagine she will be all for kissing Clint."

"That's a pretty dress," Emily chirps.

"It is a pretty dress," I agree with her as I take another dress from Amber's hands. This one is a cute floral print dress with short sleeves. Holding it against my body, the length coming to just above the knee, I wonder if Clint will like it.

"This would go well with your jean jacket," Amber points out before bending down and pulling several pairs of shoes out and mumbling something incoherent. If she digs any further, I might have to send search and rescue after her. She has too many pairs of shoes.

"You should wear that," Emily suggests between licks of her popsicle.

"And these boots," Amber says, pulling out a pair of dusty brown cowboy boots.

"You don't think it's too much?" I question as she holds the boots up against the dress. Looking in the mirror, a spark of excitement warms me, and I wonder what Clint will think.

"Not at all. Clint won't be able to keep his eyes off of you," Amber says as she peers at me through the mirror.

13

- Clint -

The image of Dawn waiting on her doorstep will forever dance in my head. Gone are her sad eyes and timid smile. Today, her beautiful smile could brighten the sky on a rainy day. The dress she is wearing hugs all her small curves showing off legs that go on for days. With her hair piled up on top of her head, pieces falling around her face, and a pair of sexy cowboy boots—she is gorgeous.

Rubbing my chest, I wonder what this constant feeling is whenever I am around Dawn. Her smile fades. I can see that all the way from where I sit in my truck watching her standing on her porch. *Crap!* I'm still in my truck gawking at her. "Right," I mutter to myself opening the door and stepping out. I try not to take my eyes off her.

"You're stunning," the words slip out of my open mouth.

"Thank you." She brightens, stepping down her porch stairs.

Closing the distance between us, I snatch her up, and crush her to my chest. Her lips are glossy and plump, begging to be kissed. So, I oblige.

Gasping, her lips part, and I enter her mouth tasting the mint of her toothpaste, while inhaling her sugary scent. It's like brown sugar and vanilla. Dawn melts into me, a small moan escapes her perfect mouth, and my dick presses hard against my zipper. Reluctantly, I pull back, resting my forehead against the top of her head. She pants into my chest. Her warm breath tortures me some more.

I have spent every day leading up to today with Dawn. I work, go to Benny's, then walk her home, where she feeds me one of her many delicious baked goods. She has a point to make. Afterwards, she lets me sample a little of her goods. I have not let it get too far. My self-control is close to breaking, but she is letting me in, and there is so much I still don't know about her.

She does not close herself off like she did before, but she still hesitates. I have also learned to avoid certain subjects, like why she moved here, and what Charleston was like so her fear will not surface because when it does, I have to reign in the urge to punch something. I have a hunch that the someone who has terrified her is back in Charleston. Even though several states lie between us and Charleston, it still drives me crazy. So much so, that I want to cross the country and lay into the man that put such fear in her. The possessive side of me wants to push her to open up, so I can protect her from whoever has her running scared. But this thing between us is too new. I will push her away if I am not careful.

"Ready?" I ask, tilting her head up. Our eyes meet. Those bewitching eyes are dark with desire. I want her eyes on me always. Helping her into my truck is a test of strength when her dress rides up showing off more of her creamy thigh. I adjust my throbbing dick before climbing in and revving the engine. I contemplate pulling Dawn across the seat, but don't because I need things downstairs to calm down.

The drive to the Fall Festival is short, filled with silence, and sexual tension. The way Dawn squeezes her legs together and clasps her hands, I know she feels it too.

"Wait," I say when I park the truck and slide out. I have never been much of a gentleman, but with Dawn, I have developed manners I never knew I had. Opening her door, I hold out my hand. She takes it, and those familiar tingles shoot up my arm and straight down to my hardening dick. *Today will be torture.*

The noise from the Fall Festival increases the closer we walk, and it gets more crowded. Dawn steps closer into my side. I don't think she realizes she is squeezing tighter onto my hand. People I know, and even some I don't, wave and smile, greeting us as we pass. It is weird. Normally, I am left alone. Some even greet Dawn. I am not sure what to think about the attention. I have been content being the reclusive mechanic.

"It's crowded," Dawn mumbles, her smile gone as she scans the surrounding people.

"You ok?" I ask, letting go of her hand and wrapping my arm around her slender shoulders.

"Fine," she says, but sounds nervous. I am not a fan of crowds either but Dawn's dislike for them isn't like mine. Her dislike is fearful. Mine is full of agitation.

"Let's go find Burns," I suggest, knowing the old man can calm Dawn's nerves.

"Amber said she'd be here with the kids," Dawn mentions.

"I'm sure we will run into them." I squeeze her shoulders, leading her toward the street where all the locals put their booths selling baked goods. Dawn snakes her arm around my waist, putting a giant smile on my face. *Yes everyone, she is mine.*

"Something smells delicious." Dawn straightens, looking around for the source. "Is that Burns?"

Looking where she is pointing, I see Miss Janet's booth. There is a line half-way down the street of people waiting for a slice of her famous cherry pie. Burns is standing next to Miss Janet with his arm around her waist and the biggest smile on his wrinkled face. "I'm not used to seeing him look so happy,"

"That line is crazy," Dawn says. "Her cherry pie must be amazing!"

"The best."

"Can we get a slice?" she asks, tilting her head back to look at me. Her fear is gone and has been replaced with excitement. Pride warms my belly, because I know I helped wash away her fear, even if it is temporary.

"Absolutely." I run my thumb across her bottom lip, tucking a strand of hair behind her ear before leading her towards the end of the line.

Before we make it, Burns' voice echoes across the line. "Yuppy! What are you doing getting in line?" Turning, I see him gestures for us to come over. "Get your ass over here."

Several people grumble as we make our way to him, but they silence their moaning when I glance at them.

"Saved you two a slice." He pulls a covered plate from the cooler.

"Thank you, Burns." Dawn reaches for the plate.

"You'll need these," Miss Janet says, handing over two forks and a handful of napkins. "I'd chat, but as you can see, I'm a bit busy."

"My woman is popular." Burns wiggles his eyes brows. "Eat up."

Dawn hands over a fork to me. She uncovers the plate revealing a large slice of cherry pie, large enough to be two slices "But what will Clint eat? There's only one."

"I didn't think you were the greedy type," I tease, pulling her close. She moves the plate out of my reach.

"When it comes to good food, I don't share." She smiles before digging in. "Oh! This is good."

"Glad you like it." Miss Janet says, while serving a customer.

"Here," Burns offers me a plate with a slice on it. "Should have known Dawn would need her own slice."

"Thanks." I accept the plate and dig in. Dawn's taking another bite, sliding the fork from

159

her lips, her eyes roll back with a moan, and I almost choke on my bite. Jesus, she can make eating food look so fucking sexy.

"Careful," Burns pats my shoulder with a smug smile.

"This is so good. I could eat this and only this for the rest of my life," Dawn says, between bites.

I know something else I would rather eat.

"Can I have the recipe?" she begs.

"Sorry, it's top secret." Miss Janet smiles with a wink, still helping customers.

"I might have to bribe you," Dawn whispers to Burns.

"I think we can come to an agreement," he whispers back.

"You two are trouble," I mutter, finishing off my pie. *Yes. I inhaled it.*

"Don't get me started on who is trouble." Burns rolls his eyes.

"Are you and Miss Janet going to be here all day?" Dawn asks, close to finishing her pie.

"Nah. We'll pack up once she's sold out," Burns answers, eyeing the remaining slices spread out over the table. "The way things are going; it may not be much longer."

"When is the pie contest?" I ask, throwing my plate away, before standing behind Dawn, wrapping my arms around her waist, and resting my chin on her head.

"Just before the Dance in the Park," Burns confirms, stepping into Miss Janet's booth. He pulls an uncut pie out. "What do you two love birds plan to do?"

"We're not love birds," Dawn chokes out, food still in her mouth. She wiggles to step out of my arms, but I hold tight. "We're not even together."

"I better get to work. You two *not* love birds have fun," he chuckles with a knowing smile.

"We'll see you at the dance," I laugh, taking Dawn's plate and fork. I scoop up the last bite before throwing it away.

"Hey!"

I grab her hand and lead her behind the booth where there aren't people walking by.

"Clint, you are being pushy again." Dawn looks adorable in her defiance.

"Just so we are clear," I say as I pull at her waist smashing her into my chest with one arm while my other hand lifts her chin, "we may not be love birds, but we are definitely together." Then, I crush my lips against hers so there is no doubt in her mind we are very much together.

14

- Dawn -

"I still don't understand why being together with Clint is a bad thing," Amber says while tearing off a piece of funnel cake and stuffing it in her mouth. We managed to find her among all the people that have crowded the streets of downtown Peak Valley. Despite the crowd of people, the Fall Festival is unlike anything I had expected. The streets are lined with food vendors, locals with their homemade goods and carnival games. I love it even though being around all these people triggers my anxiety.

"Because I shouldn't want to be together with Clint." I answer, tearing off a bite of my own funnel cake. Then, I add, "I like him too much."

"I know that feeling," she mutters. "This conversation feels déjà vu like."

"Dawn?" Emily, Amber's youngest tugs on my hand for my attention. She is the most adorable little girl. She looks so much like her mother but has the seriousness of her Aunt Sarah.

"What sweetie?" I ask, bending over to get closer.

"I read a story about Jack and his magic beans, and there was a giant. Is Clint a giant?" she asks, her eyes full of wonder.

"He is tall," I laugh, glancing at the man who towers over everyone who surrounds him. His brother Luke is the only man I know who comes close to Clint's height.

"And really scary," Emily adds, her emerald eyes wide.

"Emily!" Amber snaps. "That's not nice."

"Sorry," Emily mumbles then skips back to where her brother Matt is playing a basketball free throw game with Clint. Watching Clint with Matt melts my heart and stirs up all kinds of thoughts I never allowed myself to have. It only took seeing them together for a few minutes before I knew without a doubt Clint would be an excellent father.

"What did Sarah say when you called her?" Amber asks finishing her funnel cake and returning to our conversation.

"I haven't told her. She wasn't home when I called," I admit, finishing my funnel cake and licking my fingers. Are getting seconds socially acceptable when attending a fair, I wonder. Clint does insist I try everything and to really appreciate the food I should at least have a second helping, I conclude. Who knew frying anything makes it taste better?

"Well, I think you are overreacting," Amber says, watching Clint high five Matt after they finish their game.

"The kid swindled me," Clint announces before I can reply to Amber. It's rare to see Clint smile, but lately his smile has come out more often. Watching him ruffle Matt's hair, only tugs more on my heart strings as my forbidden thoughts begin to turn into something more. I feel it low in my belly. Emotions are different from thoughts. Thoughts you can push away but feelings tend to linger, and this feeling I don"t think will go away anytime soon. I need to tread lightly, but Clint makes it impossible.

"I warned you I was good," Matt, Amber's oldest, says as he rolls his eyes. Matt looked bored when we ran into the trio, but once Clint challenged him to a couple of games, the kid perked up. Matt has similar features to Amber, but looks more like a younger version of Benny with Amber's spirit. I have no doubt he is a handful.

"Matt said I can keep this." Emily lifts a tiny pink bear for us to see, before pulling it close and hugging it. "He *won* it."

I can tell she idolizes her big brother as her big green eyes stare up at him with fondness. I don't think Matt realizes how much she adores him.

"Can I please meet up with my friends?" Matt begs Amber while Emily is asking to go to the petting zoo.

"One at a time!" Amber cries. "Matt, yes. Go meet up with your friends, but I want a selfie check-in every hour."

"Thank you, Mom!" Matt hugs her and kisses her cheek, pats Emily's head, then takes off. The kid is fast.

"Love you!" Amber calls after him. He turns and blows her a kiss, mouthing that he loves her too. That wanting I'm trying to pretend doesn't exist grows in my belly the longer I watch Amber with her kids, making it hard to ignore.

"Wow," Clint whispers in my ear while Emily starts up her begging to go to the petting zoo. "Is this what having kids is like?"

"It's worse," Amber answers with a smirk. She teases, but her love for her kids can be seen a mile away.

"How…?" I begin.

"As a parent, you develop super hearing and eyes grow in the back of your head," Amber deadpans. I have to suck in a breath to keep from laughing.

"That's how she knows when we make funny faces behind her back," Emily adds matter of fact like. "Can we please go, Mom?"

"Yes. We will go to the petting zoo," Amber sighs. "I'll see you guys later."

"Bye." I wave as Clint pulls me to his side.

"Dawn," Amber calls out, "come see me tomorrow before you head into work."

"Ok," I call back.

"If Luke finds out you two are friends, he will want intel," Clint smirks, leading us in the opposite direction. "Make him work for it."

"I don't need to make him work for it. Amber already has that covered," I laugh while leaning into Clint's side. "Where are we going now?"

"To play Skee-Ball." He tips his head peering down at me with a mischievous smile. "Have you ever played?"

"I've played," I scoff. "Who hasn't?"

"Had to be sure." He squeezes me closer then kisses my forehead. "There seems to be a lot of things you haven't experienced."

"I've experienced things," I say, stiffening my spine. I don't know why Clint's desire to expose me to new things puts me on the defense. Maybe because the last person who tried was my mother. Or maybe because deep down, despite what my voice of reason tells me, I want Clint to show me the world, but I'm too scared to allow it.

"I meant nothing by it." Clint stops us in front of several Skee-Ball machines. He cups my face tipping my head back, so I'm forced to look at him. I'm noticed this is something he does when I'm wanting to run. "I only meant that it's your first time at a Festival. I want to make sure you experience it all."

"Including Skee-Ball," I mumble unable to relax. My voice of reason is right. I've let him get too close. He even knows how to dismantle the walls I started to build. I don't think this is what Sarah had in mind when she told me to live a little.

"Including Skee-Ball." He kisses my nose before releasing me.

"When is the Pie of the Year Contest?" I ask while Clint feeds a machine with tokens. Amber filled me in on the contest Miss Janet enters her Cherry Pie in. She had won so many years in a row, they now only let her enter every three years and this year she's up.

Amanda Lee Dixon

"We can go after I beat you in Skee-Ball." He grabs a ball from the machine and hands it over.

"Why do you think you'll beat me?" I raise my brow, swiping the ball from his hand and stepping up to the machine. "I used to be a big deal in the Skee-Ball world."

"*Used to be* being the keywords," he whispers, kissing the soft spot below my ear. "But you are a big deal in my world," he spills.

Oh.

It amazes me how with one statement, Clint is able to obliterate my feelings of fear and dread. Staring into his eyes, I know he means every word he says, and it sets off an explosion of butterflies in my stomach, kick starting my heart and warming my core. I wasn't prepared for that. I've grown used to the tingles. I've even learned to function normally whenever his touches ignite my skin and he touches me a lot. But, comments like that? Clint's upping his game. The thought is unnerving and exhilarating. Even my voice of reason is speechless as all traces of dread are wiped away.

"Getting scared?" he chuckles, still standing as close as possible without touching me.

"N-No," I cough, stepping closer to the machine, my cheeks flushed with color. I throw the first ball barely making it over the hump, winning me a big fat zero.

"Do you need a practice play?" he smirks, his eyes full of laughter and lust.

"No," I hiss, picking up my next ball and throwing it harder down the lane, this time getting forty points. My third and fourth tries hit the fifty-point bucket, but I'm still a little dazed. I need to pull it together, but Clint makes it impossible.

"Better," he smiles, stepping aside as I push him back.

Distance. I need distance so I can think and function. "I need space," I command, hoping I sound confident. "I can't have you trying to cheat."

"I don't need to cheat," he rumbles, stretching his arms wide showing me he is letting me have my space. My fifth shot lands in the fifty-point bucket. Watching, Clint looks impressed but is still smirking.

"Shit!" he mutters when my final ball lands in the 100 point bucket.

"I still got it." I smile at him, trying to hide the surprise even I have that I made the shot. "Care to place a bet?"

"I'm listening," he says, kneeling to put more tokens in the machine.

"If I win, you take Burns to brunch again," I smirk, "without Miss Janet."

"And if I win?" he asks, standing with two balls in his hand. *Jesus his hands are big.*

"I don't know… What do you want?"

Clint is standing so close now that I have to tilt my head all the way back just to see his blue eyes. They are smoldering with an intensity that makes my thighs pinch tight together.

"I want to buy you a cell phone. The kind that you can text on," he says, and my smile is gone. I step away from him and those butterflies feel like churning gnats.

"I don't need a cell phone," I mumble while that voice of reason chants 'I'm a fool'.

"I know you don't need it," he tips his head to the side, studying me. "But I want to text you and call you without having to worry about minutes."

Shaking my head, I step further from him. This is bad. Very, very bad. This is getting serious. I mean I should have known. He made it clear we were in a relationship, and I ignored it like it was just a casual thing, but to Clint it isn't a casual thing. He wants more, a get married, have babies kind of forever more, and I have ignored it. Avoided it, done everything I could to convince myself this meant nothing. I'm such a fool, a naïve fool who once again got herself in trouble with her heart, because I can't deny a big piece of my heart wants it too.

"Hold up," he grabs my wrist. I try to pull away, but it's pointless. "Don't run."

"Things are moving really fast," I wheeze out. Was I holding my breath?

"We can slow things down," he offers still holding tight to my wrist, but not hurting me. If anything, his hold on me is like an anchor, securing me, holding me still while a storm tries to whisk me away.

"That is a good idea." I adamantly nod my head up and down. "We will take things slow. No... Not slow. We should just be friends."

"I don't kiss my friends," he growls, stepping closer, his blue eyes like ice. "If you want to slow things down, I'll respect that, but we aren't friends. We crossed over that line."

"Clint..."

"Don't," he cuts me off, pulling me into his chest. He slams his lips into mine. His tongue pries open my mouth tasting every inch, stealing my breath and more of my heart. He is demanding in his kiss where before he was gentle. He's appealing to my body and my soul and drowning the voice in my head. Tearing his mouth from mine, his breath comes out as heavy pants against my face. "Do you still want to be just friends?"

I wait for the voice of reason to speak, but it doesn't so I let my heart speak instead. "No."

15

- Clint -

"May I introduce the winner of Peak Valley's Pie contest, and my woman, Miss Janet?" Burns calls out to Dawn and me. After watching the award ceremony, we managed to snag a table for us, Amber and her son Matt, whose hardly been around, opting to run around with his friends.

"Congratulations!" Dawn stands to give Miss Janet a hug.

"Congrats," Amber calls from the other side of the table. "Take a seat."

"Thank you!" Miss Janet beams as Burns helps pull her seat out.

Who knew the old man had manners? I've never seen them, and I've known him most of my life. It's like he's a whole new man, polite, thoughtful and head over heels in love.

"Oh, look there's Mrs. Bartley and the gossiping hens," Burns points out. "Ay! Mrs. Bartley did you see my woman take first again?"

Maybe he hasn't changed that much.

"Stop calling my friends gossiping hens!" Miss Janet chastises, pulling on Burns' shirt to make him sit down. "Ignore him Carol." She waves at a scowling Mrs. Bartley.

"What? It's true. They peck around getting in everybody's business." Burns says, moving his seat

173

as close to Miss Janet as humanly possible. Draping an arm over her shoulder and giving her a wink.

Dawn leans into me smiling at the couple. As the sun set earlier and the twinkle lights were turned on around the Peak Valley Park Pavilion, she began to relax, forgetting her earlier anxieties. I wish more than anything I could take those feelings away. I feel powerless when I see the spark of fear in Dawn.

"Who invited Luke?" Amber demands breaking into my thoughts. She glares daggers at Burns, then at me.

"It was Clint," Burns points his thumb my way with a mischievous glint in his eye.

"Always a liar," I groan as Luke walks up.

"Hey." Luke nods at us all stopping where Amber is seated, scanning her from head to toe. He is hopelessly in over his head with her. If he was anyone other than my brother, I'd feel for the guy. But even if Amber gave Luke the time of day, she won't be fooled twice. She will make him work for every bit of attention.

"I'm not dancing with you," Amber states, rolling her eyes and turning her attention to Miss Janet.

He is so screwed.

"Always a pleasure," Luke grumbles to Amber, running a hand through his hair. "I'm getting a beer. Anyone?"

"I'll help you," Burns offers getting up.

"I'm good," I say then squeeze Dawn's shoulder. "You?"

"I'm good," she answers tilting her head to peer up at me. Those bewitching eyes have such an effect on me. They make me want to conquer cities and slay dragons.

A local band begins to play. Soft country music fills the park; the dance is now in full swing.

"I can't believe he invited him!" Amber moans after Burns and Luke are a short distance away. She wears a look of betrayal.

"I can't believe you didn't think he would," I retort. Burns has been a schemer for as long as I can remember. If he sees an opportunity to meddle, he will. Come to think of it, he may have had a hand in the two dating all those years ago.

"He knows I can't stand Luke," Amber sighs, but watches the two men from afar. She may not be able to stand Luke, but she can't deny being attracted to him.

"Don't worry. I'll knock him upside the head for his scheming," Miss Janet claims and pats Amber's shoulder.

I hope I can see that.

"Amber, we got you a beer," Luke says holding a red solo cup towards her. Reluctantly she accepts it. "Before you toss it in my face, Burns bought it."

"As a peace offering," Burns says with a smile and a nod.

175

"I don't buy your bullshit, old man," she returns with narrowed eyes but takes a drink. "Thank you," she mutters, looking away.

"Miss Janet, I think it's time I show you my moves." Burns winks taking Miss Janet's hand, helping her up out of her chair and leading her onto the dance floor. Several other couples are already dancing kicking off the opening song.

"How's he getting home?" Dawn asks, glancing at me with concern.

"I'm taking him and Miss Janet back to her place," Luke informs us.

I wonder if Burns cleared this through nurse Cindy or if I will get a call later when he doesn't show up.

"Is that a good idea?" Amber asks, looking between Luke and I as she motions to Burns cutting the rug. "Hasn't he been sick?"

"His assisted living nurse said he needed to take it easy. He's been getting dizzy," I share with her. I trust Cindy, she has helped look after Burns for a while now, but Amber is also forthcoming with her opinion. If she thinks Burns shouldn't be dancing too much or having sleepovers, I will support it and make Luke deliver the bad news. After all, he is chaperoning the elderly couple.

"He will out-live us all," Luke puts in, turning his attention to Burns and Miss Janet who are dancing in what could be considered a provocative manner in the center of the dance floor. "That's just gross."

"I think they are cute." Dawn smiles before it transforms into a frown as she watches Burns grope Miss Janet's ass. "Ok, that is a little gross."

"You don't think they are... you know?" Luke asks, looking mortified.

"Not without help," Amber says clinically, "and if he has been dizzy, no doctor would prescribe anything."

"You make it sound so romantic," I groan not wanting to think about Burns having sex. I'm still trying to wrap my head around him having a girlfriend.

"Clint are you blushing?" Dawn asks, laughter in her eyes as she watches me.

"No, I'm feeling slightly ill," I nudge her. "Old people doing it is gross."

"You're such a weeny," Amber shoves my shoulder and both girls giggle until Burns motorboats Miss Janet while she sashays.

"Ok, that is gross," Amber coughs, finally caving in. She shifts away in her chair, only to find herself facing Luke. Swallowing hard, she turns to Dawn.

"Agreed," Dawn laughs, watching Amber turn two shades darker.

"Dance with me?" I whisper in Dawn's ear and kiss her temple. Bewitching blue eyes gaze up at me with so much emotion that I don't wait for an answer. I just pull her up from her chair and on to the dance floor.

Her hands slide up my chest, over my collarbone, and onto my shoulder. Our eyes lock and I am hypnotized by the most stunning woman to ever exist. Tingles follow the trail of her hands as my heart spikes and my stomach drops with the sensation only Dawn has the power to evoke. Thankfully my mouth is dry, and my voice is stuck in my throat because I have forgotten where we are and how new this relationship is, and I want to confess so many things to Dawn. I want to tell her she has stolen my heart, has become the center of my universe, but mostly I want to promise her protection and forever.

"Are we dancing?" she whispers, her cheeks slightly flushed. I love it when she blushes. She looks so vulnerable, not in a scared vulnerable way. No, she looks more innocent and carefree. I want to keep that look on her face more than I want air.

My hands automatically wrap around her waist, pulling her close. So close she can feel my hard dick against her abdomen. Her eyes widen and a blush creeps over her face. Smiling down at her, I sway. I'm not listening to the music and don't care what is playing. I want to slow dance with my girl. Hold her close, where I know she can feel safe.

I pushed her today. Maybe a little too far, but it seemed to work. I broke through to her, made her know she was mine. Whoever has her scared is holding her back, whispering doubt. I just have to be the louder voice.

"You look lost in thought," she says.

I could pick her voice out of a sea voices. There isn't anything unique about her voice, it's soft and low, but it's her voice and it will forever steal my attention. Dawn isn't aware yet, but I will imprint myself on her soul like she has imprinted herself onto mine. This relationship may have started off rocky, and she may still try to keep her distance, but I know these feelings I have mean something. They grow more intense the longer I'm around her. Hell, I don't even care that we haven't been together for long. My gut tells me I'm ready. I just need to convince her this is something special. More than special, legendary.

"I was thinking about earlier." I scan the surrounding dancers, noticing Amber with her arms around Luke's neck. His eyes only on Amber who is doing her best to look put off. Maybe she won't make him work too hard, after all.

"Have you changed your mind?" she asks, uncertainty crossing her beautiful face.

"No, but worried you'll run," I admit, sliding a finger up her back and down again. She shivers at my touch; her eyes darken with desire.

"You scare me," she says. This is the complete opposite of what I expected, but her eyes betray her. She is scared but not scared like most of the town is scared of me. She is scare of what this all means. I know she isn't scared of me. "Aren't you scared?"

"No." It's the truth. Nothing about making her mine scares me. Maybe it should. This is unfamiliar territory for me. I never did relationships before. I'm not even sure how to be a boyfriend, but it doesn't scare me. Her running scares me. Who she is running from infuriates me, but doesn't scare me. I'm capable of being protective. I'm protective of my brothers and Burns, but the protectiveness I feel towards Dawn is more intense, out-of-control intense—lose-my-shit-and-myself intense.

"Clint...?"

"Come home with me." It's not a question. It's filled with desperation, but I don't care. I need her to stay with me. After the barriers I broke through today, I need to keep her close, remind her she is mine, and we are together. I want to remove all her doubt and make her forget she is scared.

16

- Dawn -

We didn't stay long at the Fall Festival Dance. Clint held me close on the dance floor until I was ready to melt before leading us back to our table. Burns and Miss Janet made some excuses about an hour later, saying they needed to be home early. None of us wanted to think too hard on that and waved our goodbyes. Once they were gone, Clint thought it a good idea for us to leave as well, waving our goodbyes to a rather disgruntled looking Amber and a smiling Luke.

"Do you think you could make a better burger than Benny?" Clint asks leading me up the stairs to his loft apartment. I've never been to his place. He has always come to Benny's or my house; however, when he asked me to come home with him, I couldn't deny him. His fierce blue eyes pleading with me were my undoing. Clint has planted a seed of hope deep in my heart. Perhaps, I can make Peak Valley my home.

"I'd never try," I smile up at him. He stops at the door pulling me into his chest. His warm breath heats my face before his lips touch mine, zapping away the last of my resolve and stealing another piece of my heart. His nearness puts a speedy little beat to my heart and lights up areas of my body begging for his attention.

"Smart. I'm still waiting to be impressed," he teases as his lips hover over mine. I don't have time to response, before his kiss turns me into a pool of liquid heat, burning away all rational thought. I melt into his chest, releasing a moan of desire I wasn't aware I was capable of. We haven't even made it through the front door. Faintly, I hear the jingle of keys, before I end up against the door, my legs wrapped around his waist feeling him hard against my core. I'm not sure how it happened, but here we are and not a single alarm bell is going off.

Outside on the steps, we started slow, but now we are a frenzy of hands and tongues exploring every inch of each other. Clint has a taste of his own, tangy, and—oh, God! — he smells incredible! The more I taste, the more I want. It's like a craving I could never satisfy.

His callused hands work my dress up, pulling it to my waist where his hands continue to explore my bare skin. A shiver runs from my curled toes to the top of my head from his touch. Arching my back, I try to pull him closer. Groaning into my mouth, he pulls away searching my face. My hands clinging tight to his broad shoulders.

"Tell me to stop, Dawn," he murmurs, resting his forehead against my own, his eyes shut tight. "I can't hold back much longer."

"I don't want you to stop," I whisper, with no hesitation. I *really* want this. He pulls me away from the door and turns us towards a hallway that must lead to his bedroom. I cling tighter to his arms. Folded up in his embrace is my safe space. No fear or worry seeps into my thoughts when I'm held tight by him.

Gently, I'm laid onto a bed. He maneuvers his giant body between my legs. Holding himself up enough not to smother me, every inch of him covers me. We have too much clothing on. I want to feel his skin touching mine. His head descends as our mouths magnetize, stealing my breath and little parts of my heart. Clint's hands explore bare skin sending electric currents between my legs. He palms my breast, covering it completely causing my hips to jerk forward. His touch is too much. I can't focus as my body becomes inflamed with pleasure.

Hesitantly, he pulls back kneeling between my legs. Soft sounds escape my lips as he tentatively pushes up my dress. Gliding his hands up my thighs he stops when he gets to my hips, tugging lightly on my panties. He watches me carefully, waiting for me to give him permission. Biting my lip, I nod. My panties are gone with one quick tug.

"Your legs are fucking amazing," Clint groans as his hands spread my legs. Sinking down he kisses my inner thigh, moving painfully slow. His beard tickles me in the most intoxicating way. My whole body burns with a fiery intensity I've never felt in all my life. His breath warm against my most sensitive area has me ready to detonate when his tongue licks along my folds. It's all I can do not to scream.

I don't dare move as I teeter on the edge of oblivion. Waves of euphoria pulse through me as his tongue savors every sensitive inch. Holding tight to my hip his other hand slides a finger deep into my folds as he licks the bundle of nerves at my center. The combination is too much. Thrusting my fingers into his hair, I rock forward, coming so hard as an explosion of liquid heat consumes me.

Panting hard, he pulls away from me. My eye's too heavy to open, I hear a zipper just before the muffled sounds of his pants fall to the floor. Coaxing my eyes open, I watch him in a trance as he peels off his clothes. Opening a drawer from his bed-side table he pulls out a condom before tearing it open and quickly sheathing himself. Another new emotion settles over me as I realize I'm about to have seconds. I sit up. Clint stands between my legs, leaning forward he helps me take my dress off, his hands slowly sliding down my arms before they reach around to unclasp my bra.

"You're the most beautiful women," he whispers. The intensity in his eyes as they rove over my now naked body ignites the fire in me again. "Scoot back," he commands.

Pushing myself further onto the bed, he follows still towering over me. I lay back. He settles between my legs pressing against my entrance. Biting my lip, I slide a hand up his chest, feeling his muscles jump under my touch. My hands move up and around his neck pulling him down towards me. Our mouths meet tenderly before Clint pushes himself inside me. Too big! I let out a yelp as he fills me.

"Are you ok?" He tenses. His eyes search mine. His fingers graze down my jaw and cheekbone.

"You're too big," I whimper while I stretch to fit him. It's a good pain that fades quickly into something more satisfying. I feel full and at home, and I think this is exactly where I am supposed to be.

"Fuck! You can't talk like that," he growls, every one of his muscles tenses as he holds himself back.

"I have to move," he grates out.

Arching my back, I roll into him letting him know it's ok to move. Pulling out, he finds my mouth before gently sliding back in. He's still holding back, but I can't hold back. Pushing my hips, I rock faster against him.

"You feel so good," he whispers against my lips.

He picks up the pace. Each thrust sends a wave of heat, fanning that fire only he can ignite. There is no slowing us down as his tongue slides across my collar bone. My head falls back. He samples my neck. I let my hands explore his body, feeling the muscles as they flex with every thrust. He's pushing me closer to that edge of a fiery oblivion. I embrace it, pushing harder against his pace. Groaning loudly, I feel the scrape of Clint's teeth against my neck and it's enough to send me in a free fall over the edge. He follows, releasing deep inside me.

Clint rests his forehead against mine gasping for breath. I'm tangled in his arms. We don't move as the shock waves subside. His lips find mine, kissing me with a soft passion that has my heart skipping a beat, and he has stolen my heart and maybe my soul, with just one kiss.

"Stay with me," he pleads, searching my eyes trying to read my thoughts.

"Ok," I sigh with a smile that brightens his eyes. Rolling slowly, he pulls out of me, my once burning flesh now cold from the loss. He gets up, pulling off the condom before walking to the bathroom naked. The water turns on for a few seconds while I dive under the covers for warmth. Curling into a ball, my eyelids feel heavy. He slides into bed, pulling me into his side. Laying my head on his shoulder, I drape my arm over his waist and a leg over his thigh. Sighing, I fall fast asleep wrapped up safely in Clint's arms.

17

- Clint -

Running up two stairs at a time, I'm struck with a tightness in my chest at the site of Dawn making sandwiches, wearing nothing but one of my button-up shirts. It's a pale blue shirt that intensifies her bewitching blue eyes. She's swimming in it. Yet, she makes it look sexy. My mouth waters for a taste of her on my kitchen island. Maybe, I should take an extended lunch.

Waking up with Dawn in my arms was beyond some kind of wonderful. Listening to her breathing and watching her sleep maybe considered a little creepy, but I couldn't stop staring. She looked peaceful in her sleep, no sign of stress or sadness from whomever has her running scared. If I didn't have a backlog of repairs, I would close up shop and spend the rest of the day in bed reacquainting myself with Dawn's body and making sure she feels safe.

One taste of Dawn wasn't enough. My hands explored every inch of her while she slept, memorizing her body, while torturing my own. When her eyes opened, my mouth devoured her, with more hunger than I have ever felt. I didn't think I could wait for her to come, but then I felt her tighten around me and we came hard together.

Pulling out of her, I tell her to go back to sleep promising to return to have lunch with her before taking her home. She has a shift at Benny's Bar tonight and after my insatiable appetite, I know she could use more sleep. I always open early for customers to drop off their vehicles before they head into their 8-to-5 jobs and always staying late so they can pick them up. Maybe I should look at hiring another person, so I can spend fewer hours running the shop and more hours convincing Dawn she's mine and not much will change that.

"Are those Rueben sandwiches?" The smell of corn beef fills the apartment.

"Yes, but no rye bread. I hope wheat will be ok," she says, putting on the sauerkraut.

"I'll take whatever you make me," I whisper against her neck, my hands wrapping around her waist. Smelling my soap on her skin mingled with her brown sugar scent pushes my already wavering restraint. Gliding my tongue up her neck, I hear her suck in a breath before turning to face me.

"You make it impossible to focus," she says against my lips.

"I can never focus with you around, Sweetness," I return pulling her closer. "I doubt I can get any work done after seeing you in my shirt." Deepening the kiss so she knows just how much of a distraction she is, I kiss her long and hard like my life depends on it.

"We should eat before it gets cold," she pants against my lips. Pushing against my chest, she steps out of my embrace. I want to snatch her back toward me, but she takes another step back like she knows what I'm thinking.

Moving our plated Rueben's to the part of the island I use as the dining room table, I grab two bottles of water for us before scooting in close to her. A comfortable silence falls on us as we bite into our sandwiches. I don't know what she did to the Rueben, but it is the most amazing thing to touch my taste buds, except for Dawn.

My girl can cook. That's for sure. Still, I wasn't going to admit it. I like the playful banter too much.

"Did you go to culinary school?" I ask. I know so little about Dawn. She is a master at steering the conversation away from her, but not anymore. Things have changed between us, and I need to know more. I want to know what makes her tick, what she loves and hates, and most importantly, who has her so scared she shuts herself off from the world.

"No…" she trails off, and I think she won't say anymore. "I used to work in a bakery that also had a deli."

"You should open your own bakery, or restaurant," I say between bites. "Because you like to make food, not because it's amazing."

"Hmm," she mutters, that fearful sadness has returned. I have worked so hard to sooth away her fear, but it comes back so easily.

I take another bite, so I don't question her. After last night, I had hoped Dawn would open up

189

more, but seeing the flare of panic, I wonder just how bad her past could be. Not that it would change anything, but the need to know is eating at me.

"Have you ever thought about it?" I ask after swallowing the bite.

"Once. A long time ago," she admits; and at least, I got a little piece of information from her. "But it's not possible now."

"Why?"

"Are we playing your question game?" she asks fidgeting in her seat. She looks uncomfortable and close to tears. I struck a chord, and now she's pulling away.

"Sure." I know immediately that isn't what she wanted to hear.

"I really need to get home," she stands, but her food is only partially finished. She places it on my plate and starts cleaning up the lunch dishes.

"I'm just trying to get to know you," I say as I come around to pull her into my chest. She tenses in my arms. My stomach drops seeing the flash of fear in her eyes.

"I'm not good at sharing," she admits, looking up at me. She begins to relax in my arms before laying her head against my chest.

Kissing the top of her head, I hold her, wanting her to know I'm here and not letting go. "C-mon, go get your clothes on. I'll take you home." I nudge her towards the bedroom.

Reluctantly, she steps away with a sad smile.

I watch her walk away into the bedroom before pulling my phone out, sending a quick text to my brother Eric: *Can you talk soon?*

Waiting for a reply I mentally gather up all the things I've discovered about Dawn.

Give me 30? he replies, and I send him an *ok* just as Dawn emerges from the bedroom wearing her clothes from the day before. I don't think Dawn can look anything but beautiful.

Leading her down to my shop's office through the interior stairs, I lock the shop up and put a *Be Back Soon* sign up. Climbing into my truck after helping Dawn in, I pull her across the seat, so she's seated next to me. Revving up my truck, I throw it in gear before draping my arm around Dawn. Her small frame fits perfectly.

"I won't run," Dawn whispers so softly I barely hear her as we pull up to her house.

"Hm?" I raise my eyebrows, hoping I heard her correctly.

"I won't run," she repeats meeting my eyes. I see a confidence I haven't seen from her before. It's enough for me, more than enough. Squeezing her, I touch my forehead to hers and smile down at her.

"Good. Because if you run, I'll come find you," I tell her, pouring the truth of my words into a kiss that nearly polishes off all my self-control. I want to take her right here in my truck. I break off our kiss because Dawn deserves more than a quick lay in my truck. We are both panting hard.

Helping her out of the truck, I pull her in close, smashing my hardening length into her belly. Her eyes darken with lust, and I almost fire off in my pants. Dawn is becoming my undoing; I hope she doesn't destroy me along the way.

"I'll swing by when you close," I tell her before I step away, my cock is pressing painfully against my zipper screaming at me for letting her go. Climbing back into my truck, I hear my phone go off, and I answer while I watch Dawn enter her house.

"Hey, thanks for calling me Eric."

"It's not every day I get a text from my big brother wanting to talk," Eric returns sounding resentful, but a little curious. I'm not sure Eric will ever forgive Luke and I for leaving him to deal with Dad's death and raising Jax. Hell, I can barely forgive myself, seeing how bitter it turned Eric.

"I have...." I trail off trying to figure out how to start. "I have a situation I could use your help with."

"Is this personal or business?"

"Personal." Running my hands through my hair, I back out of Dawn's drive.

"I'm listening," Eric sighs into the phone uninterested.

"Can you look into someone for me?"

"Yeah, brother, I can look into someone. Some advice: learn from Luke and stay away from girls with questionable morals," Eric retorts with the bitter laugh he's known for. He makes it so hard to like him.

"Nothing like that. I think she's running from someone." Admitting this aloud to Eric somehow makes it real. Rubbing my chest, I take a deep breath not wanting to admit what these feelings mean because admitting these feelings when I know Dawn is hiding something is just setting myself up for a lot of pain later.

"You think she's running from someone or the law?"

"No, she's Sarah Baker's cousin," I explain. "I think Sarah brought her here to hide. That wouldn't be smart on Sarah's part if Dawn were in trouble with the law."

"Sarah's smart. She wouldn't get herself mixed up with someone in trouble. Even if it is family," Eric shares, and to my relief he sounds more serious about the situation. "It would jeopardize her career, and if Sarah is the same girl I knew back in high school, her career means everything to her."

"Whoever Dawn is running from scares her," I add.

"What other details can you give me?"

Eric seems to sense my stress, his tone starting to sound more like the Eric I used to know back when we were young, before he lost his future.

"She used to work in a bakery or deli, and I don't think she has any siblings. Her last name is Baker, and she last lived in Charleston."

"It's not much, but enough to start with," Eric states, and I hear him still scribbling down details. "Clint?"

"Hm?"

"I want you to prepare yourself for the worse," Eric states. "You may not like what I find."

The worry in his voice catches me off guard. Eric, I know has a big heart, but he had dreams, big dreams, dreams I know he thinks Luke and I spoiled for him.

"I appreciate the warning Eric. How long will this take?" I ask, trying not to sound like I'm brushing off his words of caution, but something in my gut tells me Dawn isn't someone with skeletons in her closet, at least not the type Eric wants me to prepare for.

"A few weeks."

"Weeks?" I know little about private investigation, but weeks seems a long time.

"I can get you a few details in a few days, but if you want me to paint a picture of Dawn's past, I need a few weeks," Eric explains with the annoyance back in his tone.

"Thanks Eric." I release a long breath before hanging up. This may end up blowing up in my face, but I don't care. I want nothing more than to protect Dawn, maybe even foreve

18

- Dawn -

Something is off, like when you walk into a room you've walked into many times before and you know something is out of place, but you can't place what it is. It's a chilling vibe, one I've felt before, and it has only ever led to more misfortune for me.

"No matter how many times you wipe that bar down, it ain't going to speed up time." Goosebumps prickle my skin at the man's words. Glancing up into narrowed hazel eyes, the stranger reminds me of a snake. Peak Valley is a small town and too far away from the highway for people to roll in. This man is a stranger, one who looks older from too many years of smoking taking its toll. Plaid shirt, tight faded jeans, and cowboy boots, he looks like any other person that frequents Benny's Bar, but it's his eyes that puts him out of place here. They lack the friendly small-town twinkle.

"What can I get you?" I sound uncertain. The corner of his mouth twitches, making me wonder if he can sense my unease.

"Whatever is on special," he says with a wink that sends shivers down my spine. I grab a bottle from the ice chest, pop the top off, and slide it to him. He watches my every move like a snake just waiting to make his move.

"That'll be three dollars."

"Can I start a tab?"

My stomach drops as more goosebumps prickle my skin. Normally, I start a tab for those who come to the bar. It's Benny's way of doing things, but I don't want this man to stay longer than he needs too. Warning bells are screaming at me to say no, but I nod yes before stepping away from the bar. Every fiber in my body tells me not to turn my back on him, so I side-step away from the bar.

There are only two tables occupied tonight. Benny left for the night, so he could take his wife, Linda, out for their anniversary, and since most Tuesday nights are slow, I told him I could handle the bar myself, promising I would call in help if it got busy. Now, I'm kicking myself for making the suggestion. There is no way I can call someone in when there are only a handful of customers, and they already have their food. On the other hand, I can't be alone with this man. I know it deep in my gut, but how can I call Clint without raising his suspicion?

From the corner of my eye, I keep tabs on the man. I can feel his eyes on me. I dart a look in his direction that confirms my hunch. He's observing me and it's unsettling. He downs his beer and taps the bar with yellowed fingers. He calls me over, "Hey."

"Would you like another?" My voice is higher than normal. I can hear the anxiety.

It draws out a devilish smile on the man's face as he nods.

I grab him another.

"Keep me company dear. I've had a lousy day," He claims. He's still smiling at me when I bring over another beer. He isn't ready to strike. He wants to play with his food first and watches me like I'm his next meal.

"Why was it lousy?" I ask, hearing the anxiety in my own voice. I step far enough away so he can't reach me, hoping distance will bring me a sense of comfort; although, I doubt anyone has ever felt comfortable around this man.

"Gotta a boss who keeps bustin' my balls," he says before taking a big gulp from his fresh beer. When I don't respond, he goes on. "He couldn't find no one to do this job. They all said it was impossible, but I don't believe anything is impossible. I take the job, and he has the balls to tell me I'm working too slow! Damn near lost my shit! But if I want to get paid, I gotta finish the job."

"That sounds rough," I mumble when one of my tables stands up and heads out of the bar. I take that opportunity to excuse myself, but that doesn't stop him from talking with me.

"Dear, I didn't catch your name." Turning on his stool, he watches me head for the empty table.

"Dawn."

"Well, Dawn, I'm Sal," he raises his bottle at me. "You look familiar. Do we know each other?"

"I don't think so." My heart thunders in my chest, drowning out my voice. Sal takes me in from head to toe with a calculating stare, and I think he can hear the pounding of my heart.

"Are you sure? Where you from?" he asks looking down at his nails with a smirk. He knows I'm scared of him and he likes it. He turns towards the bar again while I grab all the dirty dishes. Pretending not to hear him, I disappear into the kitchen to deposit the dishes and hopeful calm my nerves.

"Dawn, dear, where'd you say you were from?" Sal hollers through the order window that looks into the kitchen.

"Where am I from?" I repeat his question as I rack my brain for an answer.

"You don't seem like someone who's from around here," he comments, watching every dish as I separate them into their appropriate buckets. Sal doesn't want to let me out of his sight and his subtle questions aren't an attempt to get to know me. I fear he wants to pull information from me.

"I'm from here," I say, shaking my head adamantly as I walk back into the bar area.

"Everything ok, Dawn?" Clint's voice is like music to my ears, before I flush, realizing he heard my lie to Sal.

"Fine," I stammer overwhelmed by how wrong tonight is turning out to be.

Sal is eyeing Clint with a cold curiosity.

Standing only a stool away, Clint towers over the stranger. Paying him no attention, Clint seems to only have eyes for me. His gentle smile warms the chilliness Sal spread over me.

"Can I get you something?"

"Mind making me a burger?" Clint asks, taking a seat before leaning towards me fingering me to come closer. "And give me a kiss."

"Sure." I lean in placing my lips on his. He tastes like spearmint and smells like a breath of fresh air. All my fears, the wrongness of the day melts away when Clint's lips touch mine. He's my safe place, my rock, my everything. I break off our kiss before I lose myself and turn to grab a bottle from the ice chest. I hand the beer to Clint. He gives me a questioning look.

"Give me a few minutes on the burger."

I glance at Sal. His sour expression and hateful eyes send goosebumps shuddering up my arms. I pivot and head for the kitchen. I need to call Sarah, and tell her about this creep, but what do I say? That a suspicious guy walked into the bar tonight? She would tell me I'm overreacting. He isn't the only disturbing guy to ever come to Benny's. A lot of creepy guys, usually locals, have been around, but none of them had the same sense of wrongness about them.

Benny's special cheeseburgers are not complicated to make. The secret, he says, is the beef. He gets the patties from a supplier he has known all his life. I add some of Benny's dry seasoning and special mayo, and you have yourself a Benny's famous cheeseburger. Cooking or baking has always helped me de-stress. It is a task that takes me back to when my mother was alive, and we would cook or bake together. We would make up new recipes or whip up old ones. Clint coming at just the right time and the act of making up his burger is making my anxious need to call Sarah fade. *Maybe I am overreacting.*

"You two want another beer?" I ask, flashing Clint a warm smile and placing his burger before him. Sometimes, all I need in life are simple pleasures. Watching Clint take his first bite of anything I make for him is one of those pleasures, even if he doesn't admit I have amazing culinary skills. Picking up the burger, he appears friendly with his gentle smile, but there is a tenseness about his jaw that makes me wonder what he and Sal have been chatting about.

"Dawn, I'd like to buy your man here a drink," Sal declares patting Clint on the shoulder, I hadn't noticed Sal had moved closer to him. There is something unsaid going on between the two men.

I bring over two more bottles from the ice chest and clear away the empties. Sal only has eyes for me, his demeanor contradicts what his eyes can't seem to hide, the man is completely devoid of emotion. "Tell me Dawn, how does a guy like Clint get a beautiful girl like you?"

I look at Sal in horror at the subtle insult as he slaps his knee and laughs. "I'm just messing with you two kids. Don't mind me."

Clint's jaw clenches between bites.

"I should go clean up the tables. Holler if you need anything," I say, glancing at Clint.

"Sure. Don't mind us. I was just jabbering to Clint about Peak Valley. Nice town you have here," he comments as he turns on his stool and those snake-like eyes that never seem to stop watching me follow my every move.

"What did you say brought you to Peak Valley?" I ask, hoping I sound casual while I pile the dishes and trash together.

"I don't think I said." His grin looks forced. His eyes shift from me to Clint a devilish smile growing wider on his face. "Have business near here."

"What kind of business are you in?" Clint asks nonchalantly, he's almost finished with his burger and making a point not to look at me. He's just as suspicious of Sal as I am, but doing a better job at hiding it than I am.

Having cleaned up the table, I make my way to the kitchen.

"I acquire property on my clients' behalf. You know handle the more tedious, some may say, *dirty work*."

I nearly drop the dishes I'm holding at his words. Glancing up at Sal, my stomach rolls, bile clawing its way up my throat as he pierces me with a look. I don't need to ask what he means by property. I can read between the lines and see it written all over his face. Swallowing the bile, I do my best to calm my shaking hands while separating the dishes.

"Sounds interesting," Clint remarks, but Sal continues to watch me. "What property are you looking into now?"

"I have to keep that confidential. Can't give others an edge you see," he replies winking. "When you get done there dear, I think it's time I get going."

Nodding at Sal, I dry my hands. I hold on to the towel to hide my shaking hands as I ring him up and bring over his ticket. "Thanks for coming in," I squeak out.

"I like this place. I might stick around a while," he smiles as he throws cash down. "I'll catch you two kids later."

I make no attempt to collect the money Sal left at the bar. I don't even realize I'm holding my breath until the door slams shut. Looking at Clint with relief, he's frowning, that puckered scar pulls at his lip and I understand why the town fears him, he looks positively vicious.

"He was creepy," I sigh moving to collect the money, "and a poor tipper."

"I think you should stay with me tonight," Clint blurts out before walking to the door and locking it.

"Ok." I don't argue. The excited butterflies tickle my stomach as I think of being with him again tonight. Staying with Clint means feeling safe, and warm, and something else I've never felt before. "Can we stop by my place to grab some stuff?"

"Pack for a couple nights," he says, returning to his uneaten steak fries. He doesn't notice me watching him with a blush flushing my cheeks. A couple days ago, I was fighting whatever this was between us. Now more than anything, I want to be his. I want him to have all of me. It's the safest place for me.

19

- Clint -

"Can't you wash the clothes you have and stay in bed with me?" I beg like a child who doesn't want to leave the park. Dawn is tucked against me tracing shapes on my stomach. One touch from her and it's a fight for control. I turn into a caveman and want to bury myself deep inside her, making her mine, again, and again, and again.

"I need more clothes for work." Her breath is hot against my skin. She has been at my place for the last two weeks since Sal showed up at Benny's. The minute I met him; I knew there was something wrong about him. He masked his subtle insults with compliments and his prying questions were all directed at her. The caveman I become around Dawn was ready to throw him out the first time I heard him call her *dear*. I knew I couldn't let her out of my sight while he was around. There was a coldness to the man I didn't trust.

So, over the past two weeks I moved her in secret into my apartment. First with her clothes— just a few—then her laundry. When she had a day off, I convinced her to bring her mother's recipes over, so she could make me something and prove she's an amazing cook. She's phenomenal, but I'm still not admitting. I'm sure she's noticed what I'm trying to do but hasn't said anything. It gives me hope she will not blow out of here soon.

"Fine, but I want you all to myself on your next day off," I state, kissing the top of her head, then her forehead, then seeking her lips that taste sweeter than ever.

"I need a shower," she mumbles into my lips with a smile.

"And I think I need to help you wash all those hard to reach spots." Ripping the blankets from us, I roll on top of her. "You better hold on."

She doesn't need to be told twice as she wraps her arms around my neck while I pull her legs around my waist, lifting her from the bed. My apartment only has one bathroom. So, the first thing I did was have a large walk-in shower installed. I did it because of my size. I've never had a shower I could comfortably fit in. Now, I'm thanking my lucky stars I made it more oversized than necessary.

I don't let Dawn down as I step through the glass doors. Holding her away from the spout, I turn the water on before I push her up against the opposite wall.

"Oh, that's cold," she squirms pushing at my chest. The tile wall is cold against her back. Laughing, I let her slide down my body feeling every inch of her. She pushes me back towards the flowing water that steams the glass. I pull her under the stream with me. She glides her arms over my chest as the water washes over us. Turning her, I pull her back against my chest and press my erection against her back. My hands explore her body. Her head leans back against my shoulder. I pay more attention to her breasts as she lets out a moan. My hold tightens on her. She sounds magical when she's turned on.

Slowly, my hand slides to her clit as my other hand still fondles her breast. I slip a finger inside. Her moan grows louder welcoming my invasion. "Your wet," I whisper into her ear as I slip another finger inside.

"You... feel so good," she pants enjoying my fingers as they move quicker.

Her words make my cock throb for attention. Rubbing my thumb over her clit, she arches her back into me. Her hand raises up around my neck, pulling me closer. My fingers are sucked in deeper as she clamps down, dangerously close to coming hard on my fingers. I drive my movements faster, pulling her closer and closer. More moans escape her lips.

Watching Dawn come is my new favorite thing. Her cheeks flush with color as the most magical sounds come out of her. Rubbing more on her clit, I take all of her in; she's the most beautiful thing I've ever laid eyes on. Quickening my pace, I know she's close. I feel her tighten around my fingers as she shouts my name before coming hard on my hand. She's sucking in big gulps of steamy air as she melts into me with a smile. My heart squeezes every time I see that smile. I want to pound on my chest and shout, *I did that!* I put that satisfied smile on her beautiful face!

My cock is throbbing and wants me to take her now and take her hard, but I ignore it. I want to stare down at Dawn. Emotions I've never felt before. Over these last two weeks, I have done everything and will continue to do everything to make her mine. I want all of her, and I don't want to scare her with the enormity of this thing we are starting.

Dawn pulls away from me, grabbing my soap. She washes my arms, moving over my neck and shoulders, and down my chest. Her touch is too much. A bittersweet treat that leaves you wanting more, and I want more. A lot more. I take the soap from her, putting it away before turning us so she is under the water, pressing my erection into her rear. Dawn bends slightly, putting her hands against the wall. Sucking in a breath, I am close to losing all control while I position myself at her entrance. She spreads her legs apart more, I rub against her, and in one swift thrust, I am inside her. I bury myself deep, both of us moan in pleasure. I push myself as far as I can go, determined to fill her fully. Never have I had sex without a condom, but after our first shower together it became our new practice. I pull out early knowing we are playing with fire, but the act alone shifted our relationship. Even Dawn opened up more with me.

"God, you feel good," I grunt rocking into her tight pussy. She lets me take her from behind giving into my will. It is the sexiest thing, and I love it. Reaching around I rub my hand over her clit in rhythm with my thrusts. She yelps in pleasure. I feel her tighten around my cock. It makes me smile. I have nearly brought her to another orgasm. I continue my pace not relenting until I feel her clinch down and yell my name over and over as she comes undone.

Holding tight to her hips, I pick up my pace pumping harder and harder. She feels amazing. I'm so close, so very close. I should pull out to finish myself off, but I feel at home planted deep inside Dawn. I pump one, two, three more times, quickly pulling out almost too late and releasing myself onto the shower floor. My heart pounds hard against my rib cage as I hold her tight against my chest. I swear she can feel it.

"Wow," she whispers, bringing a smile to my face. I turn her to face me.

"You will be the death of me." Brushing my lips over hers, I bring her under the shower head letting the water wash over her long hair with my hands following the water down her body. *Oh, to be the water that covers her skin.*

Grabbing my soap, I lather it up gliding it over every inch of her. Dawn smells like brown sugar and vanilla, a sweetness that is her own. I love her smell but not half as much as I love my smell mingled with it.

She washes her hair while I continue to wash her body. When she's done, I wash my hair while she helps wash me down. Turning the water off, I open the steamy glass door grabbing a towel and tucking it around her before grabbing another one for her hair, and then my own.

We have established a routine over the past two weeks. My apartment and my time have always revolved around my needs, but now it revolves around us both. I've wondered if this could be what the rest of my life would look like. The more I think on it, the more I crave it. I enjoy waking with Dawn in my arms, showering with her in the mornings, and spending my free time with her. She makes the most amazing food too. Something in her sparks to life when she bakes, or cooks for me, and I have to come to love that spark. And, when we go to bed together, we make love until we are both out of breath and exhausted. It is then, when she is brave enough to open up with me.

"What would you like for breakfast?" she asks pulling me from my thoughts. She's towel drying her hair letting her eyes roam down my body. I love it when she looks at me like she's hungry for more.

"I need to check on Burns." It's been a few days since I've heard from the old man. "Let's pick up food and have *brunch* with him," I suggest.

"Can we stop by my place first?"

"I could be persuaded," I tease, pulling her in for a kiss.

While we are at Dawn's place, I watch her rummage through her closet, exasperated. "You should wear this more often." I pull out the dress she wore to the Fall Festival from her closet.

Remembering how sexy she looked when I picked her up that day has my dick twitching.

"It's getting too cold to wear it," she says grabbing it and throwing it on a small pile of clothes on her bed. There isn't much left here but clothes she can't wear in the coming winter. "Can I bring over these dirty clothes? They've sat here for weeks."

"Sure," I shrug, tucking her hair behind her ear. She looks up at me trying to hide her insecurity over the question. I know she and I should talk about all the time she's spending at my place. Women like those things defined, but Sal's visit two weeks ago is still fresh in my mind. Leaving Dawn here alone at night doesn't sit well. As far as I'm concerned, she has moved into my place. Her house is just storage.

"You don't mind? I've lived at your place for the last two weeks." She will not let this go, and I honestly don't know what to say that won't scare her off.

"I like having you at my place," I admit. My lips touch hers, tasting her sweetness. God, she tastes good. "I love having you in my bed."

"I love your bed, too. It's comfortable," she admits with her own gentle kiss.

"I don't like you here all alone," I share. I search her eyes for a hint of panic, but I only see delight. "And I don't think I'll fit in this bed."

"I don't think you will either," She laughs and it is music to my ears. Her smile, her laugh, they all trigger my heart rate to spike and a powerful urge to pound my chest when I know I'm the reason she is so happy. I lean my head down for a kiss, but she whispers, "I don't like being alone here."

My heart thumps hard against my rib cage. Her words are exactly what I need to encourage her to move in with me, and once she moves in, maybe Dawn will trust me enough to protect her from whatever or whomever she is running from.

"Then it's settled. You will move into my place." I pull her in for a hug, kissing the top of her head.

"I'm not moving into your place. It's too soon, but I'm fine with staying there… indefinitely." She smiles up at me as I roll my eyes.

"Technicality." I mutter.

Releasing me, she grabs the small laundry basket with dirty clothes. "Do you mind helping me pack?"

"Sure, I'll grab your panties," I wink, heading for the old dresser opposite her closet. It's a small three drawer dresser that has seen better days. I open her top drawer. It's empty, so I move to the next drawer, but there are only a few shorts and tops.

"Panties are in the top drawer," she says pulling a couple items from her closet.

"Are all your panties in the laundry?" I ask opening the empty top drawer again.

"No…" she trails off as she comes over to inspect the empty drawer. All color drains from her as she glances around the room. Moving over to the small dirty clothes hamper on her bed, she pulls every item out, shaking it, but no panties are there.

"Dawn?" I try to capture her attention. She looks more frightened than I have ever seen her. The hairs on the back of my neck rise.

She moves past me and out of the room towards her bathroom. I follow her as she opens a few drawers and cabinets. She even pushes the shower curtain back to inspect the tub, but there is no sign of her missing panties.

"They're gone." She shudders, coming back into the bedroom. She looks around again.

The more Dawn looks frightened, the harder I clench my jaw. My immediate thought is this has to be Sal's doing. The way he watched Dawn like he was stalking her. "*I acquire property on my clients' behalf.*"

Could she be running from someone who sees her as property? The thought disgusts me, leaving a bad taste in my mouth. More than anything I want to question her, but she is seconds from shattering before me.

"We should call the police," I try to sound calm, but on the inside, I want to explode with fury. I've never been a violent man, but in this moment, I'm finding it hard to contain my temper.

"No! No police!" she cries out and her ferocity catches me by surprise. Adamantly, she shakes her head and repeats, "No police."

"Dawn..." I trail off. My anger is long forgotten as I see her wide eyed and petrified. If

213

she doesn't want the police involved, it has something to do with her running.

"No!" she cries out again, looking moments away from falling apart.

I take a step towards her, but she steps back, and it's like being slapped in the face.

"We can't call the police."

"Ok. We won't call the police," I reassure. She looks like she can't breathe. "Calm down, sweetness." I try to coax her towards me.

"I need to call Sarah," she tries to step around me.

Blocking her, I gently pull her into my chest, ignoring the flinch, but it cuts like a knife.

"We'll call Sarah. I'll take you back to my place." I attempt to sooth her though she stays tense within my embrace. "Do you want my phone?"

She doesn't answer right away. I almost think she is ignoring me, but she relaxes a little and her arms wrap around my waist. "No. It's ok. I'll call her before I open Benny's."

"You sure?"

"Yes," she mumbles into my chest. I can still feel her pounding heart.

"Dawn?" I hesitate, weary to ask her. "You're scared of something. Whatever it is, you know I'll protect you."

Lifting her head, her tearful eyes seek mine out. Those bewitching blue eyes are a sea of emotions: desire, longing and helplessness. If I could kiss it all away I would. "I could never ask that of you."

"Then don't ask, and let me protect you," I sigh. Wrapping a hand around the back of her neck, I pull her into a kiss, cutting off any chance for her to answer. Running won't be an option for her, especially now that danger is closely lurking.

20

- Dawn -

"You're biting your lip." Clint's thumb pulls gently on my lip, releasing it from my teeth. His touch relaxes me for the moment. I have been a ball of nerves since leaving my house. We opted to skip brunch with Burns and head back to Clint's place. "Talk to me."

I don't know what to say. Sitting in his truck, I can't seem to get my words out. He deserves to know, yet I'm scared to tell him everything. Too many what ifs dance in my head. It's more terrifying than letting him still believe I'm Dawn Baker, but it's not fair and I can't do that to him. So I sit in silence wishing the ground could just open up and devour me, because telling him has become the most difficult thing I have ever gone through.

More difficult than jumping out a two-story window? Sarah's imaginary voice asks me. "Clint... I need to tell you something," I whisper, not able to look at him, tears fill my eyes.

"Who the hell?" he hisses as he gets out of the truck. Turning to see what Clint is talking about, a dark grey colored sedan pulls in behind us. I wipe my eyes and step out of the car as an impressively large man, who looks strikingly like Clint unfolds from the car. "Eric?" Their similarities are uncanny. I thought Luke and Clint looked like twins, but Clint and Eric are carbon copies. Both have black hair, watchful blue eyes and a strong jaw. "What are you doing here?"

"I came to see my big brother." Eric walks up to Clint giving him a hug. From the look on Clint's face he seems surprised but recovers quickly returning his brother's hug. I come around the truck and Eric releases him. Eric looks my way. His features are emotionless, and his eyes are cold with an intensity that rivals Clint's. His lips press together into a thin line, and I know without doubt he doesn't like me. "This must be Dawn Denton."

"How'd…" My heart is in my throat, choking me.

"I know?" Eric cuts me off, a smug smile curls his lips. He looks as scary as Clint only I really fear this man.

"Clint…" I turn with a pleading look towards the one man who has been so patient, gentle, and wonderful only to be interrupted before I can tell him who I really am. I didn't want him to find out this way.

"Don't bother," Eric gaffs. "Brother, we have a lot to talk about."

"What is going on here?" Clint looks between the two of us, taking a step closer towards me. "Why did he call you Dawn Denton?"

"Because it's her name," Eric states, putting a hand on his shoulder to stop him from getting any closer.

I wish my damn heart would stop pounding—choking my words—and just seize, letting me die here and now. I'm not sure I have the strength to share my secrets with Clint. Not while his brother stares daggers at me like I'm some kind of criminal, deceiving him.

Isn't that exactly what you are doing? Deceiving him.

"Eric let go," Clint shrugs from his brother's grasp and closes the gap between us. "Talk to me." His words are calm, his eyes gentle yet intense with a need to understand. He's comforting me, knowing I lied to him, yet he is still comforting me. That alone gives me enough hope to find my voice.

"My name is Dawn Denton," I admit. Tears blur Clint's beautiful face. "I'm not a distant cousin to Sarah and Amber. I met Sarah when she was appointed as my public defender."

"I think we need to take this inside," he wraps an arm around my shoulder, leading me towards the stairs that go up to his apartment. Tears are falling down my cheek quicker than I can wipe them away, making it impossible to read his face. Eric follows us in. He goes straight for the fridge and he pulls out a beer.

Sitting down next to me, Clint ignores his brother, tucking my hair behind my ear. I can't build up the courage to look at him. As if he could read my thoughts, his large hand pulls my chin towards him. "Nothing will change us… no matter what you have to say."

"Clint…"

"I'm serious, Dawn. I don't know your story, but I know you, and I know whatever is in your past had to be bad if it made you lie about who you are. You are not bad." His words warm my heart and make my chest feel heavy. More than anything, I want to wrap my arms around him and bury myself in his chest.

"It was Amber's idea to change my name," I tell them. The tears have stopped but still they burn the back of my eyes. My voice cracks as I continue, "Not by law because that would have left a paper trail. Sarah's plan was for Dawn Denton to disappear, and I start a new life as Dawn Baker."

"I think he's got that figured out," Eric exhales in annoyance. "I want to know why Sarah is helping you hide after they acquitted you of burglary charges."

"Eric shut it," Clint growls over his shoulder at his brother.

"Because she knows I didn't do it." I close my eyes and look up at the ceiling, sending up a prayer that Clint also believes my innocence. "I was setup."

"Setup?" Eric snickers. "If you're going to lie, at least come up with something more original."

"Eric, if you don't shut up and let her talk, I will make you shut up," Clint hisses through a clenched jaw.

"Hey, you're the one who asked me to look into her," Eric holds his hands up like he's the innocent one here.

"You asked him to look into me?" I ask him. I'm no longer worried about telling him my story because if Eric could find me, then the Port Pirates will be able too. "When?"

"A few weeks ago," he says. *A few weeks ago!*

"I have to call Sarah." Standing, I fish out my phone. "I have to leave."

"Leave?" he stands with me putting his hands on my shoulders. "Leave where?"

"Away from here." I flip open my phone, frantically trying to get my contacts to come up, *jeez this phone is slow.*

"Wait." Clint takes my phone, snapping it shut before putting it in his pocket. "Dawn, please. Talk to me."

"Yeah, I'm curious too," Eric murmurs over the rim of his beer, eyeing me with less intensity, and is that a touch of concern.

"I don't have time for this Clint. If your brother could find me under an alias then it's only a matter of time before they find me too."

"Who finds you?" Clint sounds desperate. His grip on my shoulders tightens. "Dawn, you need to start from the beginning."

"Clint, please. I need to call Sarah." Panic slithers down my spine. The need to flee is overwhelming.

"If someone is after you, calling Sarah may be what they need to pin-point your location," Eric says as he comes around the love seat and sits down. "Take a seat. Right now, Sarah can't help you, but I can. Only if you tell me what you are up against."

"Dawn, you promised no more running," Clint whispers into my ear, pulling me into his chest and sitting us down.

"I never meant for this to happen," I murmur into his chest.

"I know," he says softly into my hair. "You fought me every step of the way."

"You should let me go." I try to push him away, not wanting to fall into his safety only for it to be wrenched away.

"Let me be the judge of that," he insists. He holds me tight, his hand fists in my hair before his lips touch softly to my forehead. "Please stop fighting this."

"I don't know where to start," I sigh, looking over at Eric who has watched us in silence.

"Start with the men who are after you. Who are they?" Eric suggests, pulling a note pad from his back pocket. It is one of those note pads I have seen police officers carry around jotting down details.

"They are part of the Port Pirates Motorcycle Club in Charleston, South Carolina." I answer. Maybe it was Clint's kiss or the plea in his voice that stole the last of my resolve... or maybe I am tired, tired of running, tired of looking over my shoulder, tired of not being able to plan for a future that would allow my walls to drop. "My ex, Darin, stole from them. How much? I don't know, but it was a lot. Enough that they won't quit looking for me."

"When did this happen?" Eric asks, scribbling away not looking at me. His eyes on his note pad make it easier to answer his questions.

"Almost two years ago," I say, my voice flat, as I retell my story. I have told it so many times I could say it in my sleep, but with each telling only one person seemed to believe me, Sarah. "I never knew about the criminal activities Darin and his MC were part of. I thought it was a bunch of guys riding together up and down the coast of Charleston."

"How did you find out about the criminal activity?" Eric asks, still scribbling away. His handwriting is not legible, but it comforts me. Everyone else I told my story to barely wrote anything down, and when they did, it was vague and seemed irrelevant.

"After I was arrested, Sarah put it together."

"Did Darin show you the money he stole?"

"No, he disappeared. Sarah thinks he stole the money and skipped town," I say glancing at Clint. His features offer no comfort until he squeezes me softly. Even under stress, his intimidating stare doesn't scare me.

"So, Darin steals from his club, disappears, then what?" Eric prompts, scanning through his scribbled notes.

"Several of his MC friends would call, ask me how I was doing, and even come see me at the bakery. This went on for several weeks until I called Darin in as a missing person. He had no family. We both grew up in the foster care system. That is how we met. His MC buddies were pissed when they found out about the missing person report. A few days later my apartment had been broken in to. My stuff was thrown around. They tore my couch, and my bed was ripped apart, but they stole nothing."

"What did the police say?"

"Nothing. It wasn't a priority. Nothing was stolen, and they didn't think it was connected to Darin's disappearance."

Taking a deep breath, I rub my temples, a dull headache had set in. "I'm convinced Darin is dead. He would not have just left without an explanation, but his MC buddies think he's living off their money on some beach in the Caribbean. Sarah thinks he is still alive, too."

"And they arrested you not long after the break-in, correct?" Eric asks, looking up from his note pad. His eyes fall on Clint assessing him quickly before shifting his gaze towards me.

"Yes, about a month later." I suck in a deep breath before launching into the darkest time of my life. "They arrested me for *supposedly* stealing a diamond ring. The owner of Digger's Pawn Shop swore he bought it from me, but it wasn't me."

"How can they arrest you based on some guy's word?" Clint asks, his voice tight with tension.

"The owner turned it in missing, and someone tipped the police off that it was at

Digger's Pawn Shop," Eric explains to my relief. "That was enough to charge Dawn."

"That is all it takes?" Clint growls, pulling me closer to his side. The small gesture soothes some of my tension and settles my nerves. He isn't pulling away but pulling me close.

"The evidence was pretty convincing," I breathe out, remembering Sarah going over the testimony from the pawn shop owner. "Sarah proved it wasn't me though."

"How?" Eric asks but I think he already knows the answer. He wants to hear my version, the version you cannot read on some public document. Eric like Sarah seems to have that uncanny ability to know when someone is lying or not and he is testing me.

"Sarah found footage of me working at the bakery during the time someone stole the diamond ring, and when it was sold to the pawn shop."

"The pawn shop had no footage?" Eric questions looking unconvinced, still assessing me.

"It was over written."

"So, you were free to go. Is that when you moved here?" Eric asks, moving us along, his test over. Whatever the results I may never know, but at least he isn't glaring at me with eyes like Clint's.

"No. Not long after they dropped the charges, I received threats. My car was broken in to, and weird complaints were being made against me at the bakery. I lost my job. Sarah had me go to the police, so they could look into it. They didn't think I had a stalker, but they also didn't believe it was the Port Pirates, so nothing was done," I share. My throat is dry like I have been talking for hours. Exhaustion is setting in, and it is barely mid-afternoon. If the Port Pirates don't take me out, stress will. "I found another job at another bakery, as far away from the Port Pirates as possible. I was thankful for a job. I didn't care that it sold cheap bread and stale cupcakes. Sarah helped me move into a new apartment closer to my new job, and she put it in her name. For a while it was quiet."

"Until?" Eric asks not looking at me, focused on his writing.

"Until the Port Pirates sent someone to kill me."

21

- Clint -

"Thanks, Eric. I owe you." I shake my younger brother's hand as he heads out the door.

"I haven't done anything yet, but I'll give Sarah a call and fill her in on everything. Tell Dawn to cut all communication with Sarah. From now on, she needs to go through me." He points at me as he backs down the stairs. "I'm serious Clint, take her phone if you have to."

"Got it," I salute and shut the door. I turn around to see Dawn in the kitchen making coffee. Her petite figure looks fragile and those bewitching blue eyes are swollen from crying. The deep sadness steals her radiance. "Come here, Sweetness."

Tentatively, she moves forward, carrying two cups of coffee, she closes the space between us. Taking a cup with one hand, my other hand curls around her waist, pulling her close and breathing in her sweet scent. The protective part of me wants to erase the look of sadness in her eyes because Dawn is not meant to be sad. She is the kind of women you build your life with and have babies with and grow old with. She is my ticket to a happy ending.

"You are so calm about everything," she states, leaning her head against my chest.

"I'm good at concealing rage," I breathe into her hair, rubbing a hand up and down her back. Tipping her head back, she looks up at me, searching my face, but I don't let her see what I'm feeling or what I wish I could do to the men that have hurt her.

"I'm sorry," she says for what must be the millionth time. She has nothing to be sorry for. She is not a burden, but I get why she thinks she is. She runs a finger across my bearded jaw. She pulls her coffee to her lips, sipping it as those bewitching blue eyes still search my face.

"Stop apologizing," I whisper. Her eyes draw me in. Even the way she sips coffee is sexy. Her nearness always heats me up. The brown sugar and vanilla scent that clings to her intoxicates me, thinning my restraint. I need to feel her, be inside her, reassure her that I am here and will protect her. She is mine. Always mine.

"Clint…"

I cut her off with my mouth, kissing her hard. She breaks away putting her coffee down. I do the same before possessively pulling her in and making her mewl with a deep long kiss. Wrapping my hands around her hips, I lift her up. Her legs circle around my waist. Her arms cling tight around my shoulders.

Carrying her down the hall to our room—yes, our room, because this is where she will stay, always—I stumble, trying to find the doorknob as I taste her sweet tongue. In my bed—no, *our* bed—I need her next to me, safe, and loved. Yes, loved. Because these feelings I know we both have are big and indescribable. They consume us. They propel us towards something indestructible and infinite.

She tugs on my shirt and lifts it over my head before I lay her down on our bed. We both kick off our pants, and I help her take off her shirt and bra. Standing over her naked body, I stare down at my forever. My chest is heavy with emotion. Leaning in, I place soft kisses on her stomach. My fingertips trace her side as I make my way up. Her chest rises and falls anxiously as if it can barely contain our shared feelings.

I run my fingers over her nipples, my mouth waters as I feel how hard they are. I need to taste them, pulling one into my mouth, she moans as her back arches. My hard cock twitches against her thigh, begging to be inside her. Releasing her breast, I move onto the other one, showing it equal attention. Her legs wrapped around my waist pulling me in more. She whimpers as my cock brushes against her folds. She is getting loud and desperate.

I can't hold back any longer. The noises she is making will be my undoing. Rubbing the head over her clit—one, two, three times, I slide deep inside her. We both cry out as we become one. Her walls tighten around my cock. Her fingernails dig into my shoulder. The need to release is so powerful I almost can't hold back.

"Clint…"

"Jesus! you feel amazing," I hiss through a clenched jaw, taking a deep breath. I drop my forehead against hers and pull her arms above her head. I need a moment. She stills beneath me; her tight warm walls ripple in anticipation. I suck in another breath.

"Are you ok?" she whispers into my ear, kissing my jaw then my lips.

"I need a moment," I lift my head, searching her face. She must see my strain. Her eyes soften. Pulling her hands from my grasp, she frames my face and places a small kiss against my lips.

"Make love to me," her bewitching blue eyes beg as they darken with desire with a need only I can understand.

"Fuck!" I growl, pulling out and sliding in again, hard. Our pace is urgent with need as she steals my breath, my heart, and my soul. Her legs tighten around me as I thrust faster, neither of us looking away. Unspoken words and promises fuse us together.

I feel her ready to orgasm as my own climbs up my spine. I plunge deeper, and she cries out my name. Her fingers are tangled in my hair and everything blurs around me. A primal roar erupts from my throat as I release deep inside her. Blinding stars dance in my vision. I feel light-headed. I rest my head against her chest, and I can feel her heart racing.

"I'm falling for you," I barely hear her whisper.

"What?" My head shoots up, making me dizzy. I seek her eyes, but she has turned her head, not wanting to look at me. Framing her face with my hands, I gaze into her eyes. They stare down at my mouth, her lower lip trembling. "Look at me, Dawn," I whisper.

"I can't," she chokes out as a tear slides down her temple.

I brush my thumb under her eye. "Look at me," I coax, trying to get her eyes to catch my own because when I tell her how I feel, I want to look into her bewitching blues eyes. Her eyes flick up catching mine, stealing my breath because there lies raw emotion equally powerful as my own. "I've already fallen."

Her eyes widen, but she says nothing. My heart skips a beat and then her mouth is on mine. Her tongue slides against my lower lip, and I open for her. Our tongues tangle in a frenzy, and my cock twitches inside her ready to make love to her again. We let our bodies say, *I love you* with unspoken words.

*****

"It's been three days, Eric," I exclaim as I slam the hood of the car I'm working on, "and you still have nothing?"

"Clint, these things take time." Eric tries to calm me down, but I see the flash of annoyance cross his face. "We have little to work with."

"So, we wait?" I growl, glaring down at my greasy hands as I try to wipe them clean with a rag. "For how long?"

"For however long it takes," Luke chimes in, and I want to punch him.

Why did Eric have to get him involved? The last thing I need is my cocky older brother to charge in and take over. Him and his hero complex, so far, has only pissed me off even if he is helping to keep an eye on Dawn. What I need are answers. Something that can help piece together who and why someone is after Dawn.

Darin going MIA or being dead, hopefully in a ditch somewhere, sheds no light on the situation. Sal hasn't shown up at Benny's since the night we met. This leads me to think he really isn't involved, but someone stole Dawn's panties, and that *someone* is a threat. One I intend to take out.

"Clint, I know this is hard waiting, but whoever is after Dawn is patient. They are waiting for the opportune time to attack. We have to stay on guard until Sarah and I can figure this mess out." Eric pats my shoulder, and I find it patronizing. Shrugging his hand off, I go for my beer fridge. I pull out three bottles and pass them out. I need to calm down and make amends with my brothers. I direct my frustration toward them because I have nowhere else to direct it.

"We can't babysit her forever," I sigh, letting my shoulders relax a little. Dawn is already at Benny's working her shift. With Benny on duty, the three of us have the rare chance to talk in private. Not that I want to keep anything from her, but she doesn't need to see my frustration or know that getting to the bottom of this shit has stalled out. "I feel like she left one prison just to land in another, and I'm the one keeping her locked up."

"You aren't holding her hostage, Clint," Luke says, holding the bottle to his lips. "You are protecting her. There is a difference." His eyes blaze with the certainty in his words as if talking from experience.

I don't want to ask. I know he has seen nasty things while in the service.

"Clint, I have an idea," Eric says, looking down at his beer. Sighing he looks at me with a pained expression. "You won't like it."

"I'm listening." I hesitate before taking a long chug from my beer.

"I think whoever is after her is trying to get her to run," Eric begins. "The visit from Sal… you said he made subtle threats, and when that didn't work—the missing panties."

"This sounds more like a theory," I note with narrowed eyes.

"When Eric has a theory, he usually has a test to prove his theory," Luke mutters, eyeing Eric suspiciously. "And the test usually isn't the safest option."

"I get results. Don't I?" Eric retorts, glaring at Luke. "If I'm right, maybe we need to set up a scenario where Dawn looks vulnerable. We could lure whoever is behind the theft out from hiding and get to the bottom of things."

"Are you suggesting we use Dawn as bait?" I hiss, squeezing tightly on my bottle. A reddish tint clouds my vision, and brother or not, I might kill Eric for even thinking about putting her in danger.

"I would never put her in the path of danger, but yes, I think we should use her as bait."

"I think you should go fuck yourself!" I growl, throwing my bottle into the trash. It shatters from the force. Beer sprays the trash can as the glass falls, and I walk away before I do something idiotic, but justified.

I promised to protect Dawn, not serve her up on a silver platter.

22

- Dawn -

I am surrounded by men. A lone woman in a proverbial meat locker. I think none of them have realized it either. They keep pulling me into their conversations over whether the Chiefs will make it to the playoffs this season, or if anyone heard about someone's new truck? Sometimes I really don't get men.

"Dawn tell Benny the wind we've been getting is from the ice caps melting," Burns hollers over at me. It's been mostly dead this afternoon, and I don't expect many people to come in tonight. "She'd know. She is young and knows the internet."

"Burns the wind is no different than it was when you were a boy," Benny argues while he mops up the beer Burns keeps spilling from his glass. The old man shakes something fierce when he gets riled up and today, he is riled up.

"Oh bother, you don't know what you're talking about," Burns waves away in disappointment.

"Thursday, it should have a lot of wind," Marty, a regular, chimes in two seats from Burns. "Friday, too!"

"I'm telling you these winds are picking up in speed," Burns turns to his new ally.

"You know they say Tornado Alley shifted," Marty tells Burns. "It's why we haven't seen no tornadoes in a while."

"What does that have to do with the ice caps melting?" Burns looks incredulous at Marty before rolling his eyes and turning my way. "I'm surrounded by idiots."

"Burns why are you so cranky?" I ask with a smile only for Burns because I know there is nothing but my smile and Miss Janet that can turn Burns' mood into something less hostile.

"Miss Janet's having lady's night with the gossiping hens," Burns mutters into his beer. I do my best to hide my smile. He hates it when I act *girly* about their relationship. It is hard not to. They are the cutest oldest couple.

"Jealous?" Benny asks with a smirk and a wink towards me. Benny loves to rile Burns up. I get why, though. The things that come out of Burns' mouth either make me laugh, cringe, or cry.

"Benny!" someone cries out as they crash through the entrance door. The man doesn't look familiar, not a regular, but it's hard to tell with him bent over one hand holding his side, the other on his knee. He's taking deep breaths as if he ran a long way to get here.

"Ted, what are you fussing about?" Benny furrows his brow as he comes around the bar to meet the man. "Dawn grab water."

"Benny, you got'da come quick. Your house is on fire!" The man huffs between pants, his face is red as sweat drips from his forehead.

"My house?" Benny asks looking confused.

"No, your old place." the man corrects as he stands up to his full height. He's a heavier set man, at least twice Benny's size around and half a foot shorter. "I came running when I saw the fire department pulling up."

"My old place… by Amber?"

"Yeah!" The man wipes his face before thanking me as I give him a glass of water. Benny eyes me before placing a hand on my shoulder.

"Dawn, I need to go check things out."

"Oh God, Benny," I choke out. Ted is talking about my place. The small house Linda and Benny Baker let me rent out. The house Sarah and I spent a week scrubbing clean. Clint kissed me for the first time on that porch. With everything going on, I haven't told Benny I moved out of there, and now it's on fire. A cold sinking feeling turns my legs into jelly.

"It will be ok. You stay here. I'll go check it out." Benny puts his hands on my shoulders, and I almost crumble under the weight. Leading me to a stool behind the bar, he asks, "Can you manage everything?"

"I'll stay with her," Burns calls over before I can answer. Benny releases his hold on me, his emerald eyes filled with concerned. I watch Benny share a glance with Burns. Unsaid words pass between them.

"If I'm not back in an hour, close the bar. I'll call Clint when I've got something to report back on," Benny tells me.

Automatically, I nod, but I'm only half listening. The fire isn't an accident. It's another warning, and I know what is coming next.

Ted follows Benny out the front entrance. The fading sunlight splashes the dreary bar with light before the door slams shut.

Marty stands and throws a few bills on the bar. "I'll get out of your hair, Dawn."

I wait for Marty to leave before rushing to collect Marty's glass and money. "I've got to get out of here," I hiss to Burns. Scrambling, I shove the money into the register.

"Dawn, you need to calm down. Take a seat for a moment," Burns returns with a nervous concern I've never seen before. "I'll call Clint and have him come over, but let's not jump to any conclusions just yet."

"Burns you don't understand! I'm not jumping to conclusions. I know it will be bad," I plead. Burns doesn't know the truth about me. He doesn't know that being around me is putting his life in jeopardy, and if something happens to him, it would be all my fault. After everything the Baker's, Burns, and Clint have done for me, I can't put them at risk.

The entrance door opens. Faded sunlight now nearly dark barely brightens the bar as Burns and I watch in anticipation, only for it to turn to sour nausea. "Just my luck!" Sal greets with a slippery smile. "I was hoping, I'd get to see you."

"Who are you?" Burns spits out with a scowl on his wrinkled face. Sal must give Burns a bad taste in his mouth too.

Ignoring Burns, Sal's murky hazel eyes never leave me as he makes his way to the bar. Taking the seat closest to the end, he could block my exit.

"Burns, this is Sal." I say with a shaky voice. This can't be a coincidence, Sal showing up at the same time my house catches on fire.

"Don't get too comfortable. We are closed." Burns narrows his eyes on the man who still holds me hostage with his stare.

"Dawn and I are friends. I'm sure she will let me have a beer before she closes up." Sal comments not sparing a glance for Burns.

Feeling like a cornered animal, I slowly stand. My legs feel as if they may give out at any moment. I step towards the ice chest and pull out a bottle. My mind goes blank with fear. Sliding the bottle towards Sal, I can smell the cigarette smoke on him, and it makes me want to gag.

His yellow hands grab his beer, and he chugs it hard. "Man, I'm thirsty!"

"Finish up quick. We want to get out of here," Burns growls. He stands and snatches up his half empty bottle. Walking around Sal, he glares at the back of his head. Coming around the bar, Burns plops down on my stool. Sal can't avoid Burns now. Not with him sitting directly in front of him.

"Old man, Dawn and I are friends," Sal says with a clenched jaw, his eyes casually sliding towards Burns. Annoyance radiates from him.

"You ain't no friend of mine. Now hurry up, and get lost," Burns orders, clenching tight to his bottle. I can see the slight shake of his hands. I wish I had a real cell phone right now. Not the ancient flip phone that takes an hour to send a simple text. With a real cell phone, I could text Clint, tell him to come now and save me from this snake.

"Why are you closing so early?" Sal directs the question at me.

Feeling light-headed, I realize I've been holding my breath as my heart pounds in my ears. "Fire at Benny's old place," I say. Sucking in air and the putrid cigarette smell that has invaded the bar. I almost heave. I've got to get out of here.

"That's too bad," Sal says with a knowing smile.

"Dawn?" A deep, beautiful voice calls from the door. Relief floods my numb, immobile body, jump starting it back into existence. I don't even hesitate as I pass Sal. I run into Clint's waiting arms.

"Clint!" Sal's greeting lacks enthusiasm as he lifts his empty bottle. "Come have a beer with me."

"Didn't expect to see you again," Clint replies. His features lack any trace of emotion, but his hold on me is protective.

"Funny how business keeps putting us together," Sal laughs. His smile looks forced. His eyes snap back to me.

I'm clinging tightly to Clint's side, not wanting to let go.

"How about another beer?" Sal says.

"We're out," Burns snarls, looking fierce behind the bar.

Sal doesn't turn his attention but keeps it focused on me. There is a cruelness to Sal's features. He hides it behind a mask, but his mask is chipping the more Burns denies him. "Fine, fine," Sal sniffs incredulously. "I can tell when I'm not wanted."

Clint pulls me towards the bar as Sal stands. Pulling his wallet out, he throws a crumpled bill onto the counter. "I'll be seeing you," he says to me, his vicious smile taunting me.

I've got to get out of here.

23

- Clint -

Arson is what the Fire Chief told Benny he suspected but can't confirm until after the investigation is complete. In my gut I know it this had to be Sal's doing. The bastard set the house on fire, hoping it would leave Dawn alone at the bar. I have no proof, and law enforcement won't listen to gut instinct, but I know it was his plan. Deep in my bones, I know Sal was responsible for it.

"What time is Sarah and Eric getting here?" Dawn asks from the kitchen where she's cleaning up our lunch mess. I should help her, but since the fire, my thoughts have been borderline murderous. I'm ready to hunt Sal and every Port Pirate down.

"Probably not for another hour," I grunt from the balcony window, watching over the salvage yard. To most it looks like a heap of garbage. Wrecked cars sit crushed in piles. Old tires line pathways through the junk. It's my treasure, endless rows of tinkering projects and car parts that will help my customers spend less. I look over the yard when I'm stressed. Something about it is calming. Like watching time stand still while I collect my thoughts.

"Clint?" Dawn calls, her voice a little shaky. Turning she looks hesitant, and a little nervous. I will take that look over her fearful sadness. "I've

243

been thinking maybe I should take Eric up on his offer."

"What?"

"I need to get out of here," she pleads with her bewitching blue eyes. Those eyes pierce my soul while her words salt the wound. "How many more people have to suffer because of me?"

"Running isn't the answer, Dawn. I thought we covered this," I try not to roll my eyes, but I doubt I can hide my annoyance.

"I can't sit here and watch anymore people I care about get hurt," she snaps, tears threatening to spill down her creamy cheeks. "I see what it is doing to you, too."

"I asked you once not to run. Now, I'm asking you to promise you won't run," I say to her as I cross the room to stand before her, never cutting eye contact. My annoyance disappears as I get close because she needs to see me stand strong and not angry even if I feel powerless.

"The Port Pirates tried to kill me. I'm scared they will try to kill you," she sounds desperate. She begs for me to let her go, but she must know that I can't. I'm too far gone, and nothing will tear us apart.

"Tell me you don't feel this connection?" I cut in. "Tell me this thing between us isn't worth protecting."

"I… It's not that simple," she stutters, but I know she can't deny it.

"Nothing ever is, but I will fight for this." I pin her with my eyes. "Tell me this isn't worth fighting for, and I will let you go.

"It's worth fighting for!" she chokes out with a sob in her throat as tears fall like little streams, twisting my heart. I hate seeing her cry. "But at what cost?"

"At what cost?" I repeat. Wrapping my hands around her face, my thumbs wiping away the tears escaping from her beautiful eyes.

"The cost of losing you. Losing us. I rather know you are alive than live with knowing I am the reason you were killed."

"Have more faith in me. The Port Pirates don't scare me. Trust me to protect you." Leaning my forehead against hers, I need her to trust this and fight for this. Am I asking for too much? There is no question in my mind that I am in love with her, but Dawn is fearful, guarded. Maybe I am expecting too much.

"I trust you," she sighs, leaning into my chest as her arms slide around my back, and in one quick motion, I lift her up in my arms. Her legs wrap around my waist, as I seek out her lips. I needed to taste her. We explode into a frenzy of passion, her hands are everywhere, tugging at my shirt, while her core presses hard against my erection. It's almost too much. I need to be inside her, now. My body has a mind of its own and carries us into the bedroom while I kiss and nibble on her lips.

Dawn has my shirt and hers off before we make it to the bed. Laying her against the bed, I find her zipper and slowly pull it down. Sliding her jeans off, I leave a trail of kisses as I slow the frenzy. I watched her get dressed this morning; I know what lays beneath her clothes, but damn it if it doesn't suck the air from my lungs when I see her lacy panties.

"Mine," I whisper, taking in every inch of her.

Pushing up on her elbows, she unbuttons my pants. Her hands sending lightning tingles through my body. Dropping my pants, she sets herself back down on the bed before I cover her with my body. Wrapping her arms around my neck, she pulls me down and kisses me with an intense need before pulling back to search my eyes.

"Make love to me," she whispers softly.

I almost didn't hear her. Her body is shaking beneath me. Looking deep into her bewitching blue eyes, I don't even realize I'm pushing up against her entrance until I thrust forward. Her breath hitches as she calls out my name.

"I love you, Dawn," I say, unable to hold back my feelings. Her body surrounding mine feels right, like two halves coming together as one, and I want to hold on to this feeling forever.

"I love you," she whispers back. Her arms clinging tighter around my neck, she seeks my mouth. Passionately kissing me, she uses her body to tell me how she feels. I want her to know how I feel. I've never said those words to another woman in my life, so I show her with my body.

We start off slow, making love to each other. Exploring with our hands, and mouth, but the emotional pull has us picking up the pace, grinding against each other. Sliding in and out, she's wet and warm. It only makes me harder. My arms clamp around her, holding her tightly as we meet thrust for thrust. I feel her insides tighten, and I'm not sure I can hold back much longer. I whisper my love to her over and over. She pulls me hard inside her so deep that I see stars and her orgasm rips through her as I release hard right alongside her.

We stay wrapped in each other's arms panting for several minutes. I want to stay right here with her forever where her fears don't touch her. "You love me?" I ask gliding my hand down her cheek.

"Yes, I love you," she tells, her lips brushing against mine. "I knew you were different the moment we met."

"I think I fell in love with you the moment I saw you," I admit, searching her eyes for that sadness she tucks away. "You looked up at me with your beautiful eyes, and I knew whatever it was that made you look sad, I would protect you from."

24

- Dawn -

"Absolutely not!" Clint cries out as he stands up from the couch. He paces. His expression darkens. "I told you once already, Dawn won't be used as bait!"

Sarah arrived a few hours ago wanting to know everything that has occurred since she left a few months ago. Thankfully, Clint and Eric do most of the talking. Recounting the fire that caused those never-ending tears to prick at the back of my eyes and made me wonder if I will ever get over the guilt. The fire not only blazed through my house, it partially burned down Amber's house next door. Now, her and her two kids are back to living with Benny and Linda. Sarah is staying in a hotel but has mostly been with Clint and me trying to sort out the mess instead of being with her family.

"Luring the bastard out is our only option at this point," Eric stresses, he looks more tense than ever. When we first met, I thought he was an arrogant egomaniac with a chip on his shoulder. These past few days have shown me it is just a mask he likes to wear. Beneath his superficial persona Eric is just as gentle and caring as his brother Clint.

 the😀

"By putting her in danger?" Clint roars, his pacing increasing in speed. "Come up with another idea!"

"I agree with Eric. We need to lure this Sal character out," Sarah tries to sway Clint, but he only deepens his scowl. Sarah flinches before adding, "We have enough circumstantial evidence to leverage against them."

"Just like that you think these Port Pirates or Sal will just stop?" Clint spits out looking doubtful. If I didn't know Sarah as well as I do, I probably would have doubted her too, but she knows the law and she has one hell of a backbone.

"All we have to do is convince them that Dawn knows nothing about the stolen money, and if things keep escalating, launching an investigation into the Port Pirates would be an easy sale with the authorities," Sarah explains. Her eyes drift slowly towards me, silently asking my opinion.

"Clint…" I begin, but I trail off when his eyes like a winter storm land on me. His features soften, only for me, as he stops his pacing. "I think we should try it."

"Try it?" he repeats and presses his lips together in a thin line. At least the bitterness in his tone has softened.

"If anyone can convince the Port Pirates I had nothing to do with the stolen money and threaten to expose them, it is Sarah. I trust her," I plead. My stomach turns to knots. Even if Sarah believes we can do this, the plan makes me nervous, but I owe it to her to try. After everything she has done and what her family has sacrificed, sitting around doing nothing isn't an option.

When I came to Peak Valley, I wasn't looking for anything but a place to hide. Thoughts of a future were not something I allowed myself to have. I never thought I would have a future. I had no intentions of ever being in a relationship again. How could I when it would only put them in danger? Yet here I am with Clint who loves me. He refuses to let me run and promises a future. He has given me a reason to fight back.

"Sarah is putting herself at risk, too," Eric points out which lands him another glare from his brother.

"Eric is right," I chime in after several awkward seconds. Sarah is putting herself at risk, she is going to great lengths to pull me out of this mess. In the beginning the Port Pirates only wanted to hurt me, but their last stunt affected Benny and Amber. I'm scared their next stunt will be even more devastating. "You asked me to stop running, to trust you to protect me, and I am, but the longer I hide behind you the bigger the target on your back gets."

"I don't care how big the target gets," Clint growls in frustration while pinching the bridge of his nose.

"I care! It's not just you who could get hurt next time," I counter. I hate upsetting him like this but if anyone will get through to Clint, it will be me. "What happens when he attacks Eric or Burns?"

He ignores my question. "And if Eric's plan doesn't work?" Clint counters, stepping towards me. Pinning me with his eyes that smolder with a desperate madness, he breaks my heart. He towers over me like a giant looking lost as he whispers, "I just found you. I can't lose you."

"We will be there to make sure it works," Sarah says somewhere in the background, but both of us ignore her.

He pulls me up from the couch, tugging me into his chest. Too many unsaid words are passing between us as I try to convey my faith that we will get through this. "If anything happens to you..." he murmurs into my hair.

Pressed against his chest, I can feel his heartbeat. It's steady and true and I know I am safely locked in it. I wish I could reassure him right now, but if I want forever with him, I have to fight back. Pulling from his embrace, I turn to face Sarah and Eric. "What do I have to do?"

*****

"We will be back tomorrow to go over the plan again," Sarah says with a hug. Eric plans to take her to her parent's house to check on her family, before heading back to the hotel. Sarah insisted she would be fine, but Eric insisted on a buddy system. He also can't seem to take his eyes off her, while Sarah keeps blushing around him. I have never seen Sarah blush before. If I wasn't so wrapped up worrying about Clint and his constant pacing over my decision to fight back, I might try to get the scoop on the two but right now Clint needs me.

"I work tonight and tomorrow," I remind her. With Benny busy dealing with the aftermath of the fire, it only seemed fair to make sure the bar was open, clean and ready for business. It was the least I could do. I should call Amber and see how she is holding up, but I don't know what to say, or even where to begin. "Is Amber ok?" I blurt out before Sarah steps out the door.

"She will be fine," Sarah sighs with a sympathetic smile. "It isn't your fault what happened."

"My mess, my fault," I grumble, looking away.

"Dawn don't beat yourself up," Sarah orders, squaring her shoulders in front of me. "You didn't ask for this. You did nothing, so stop holding yourself accountable."

Nodding, tears prick my eyes and clog my throat. Clint comes up behind me and says his goodbyes before closing the door. Turning he looks down at me, his blue eyes are like ice filled with a desire and a helplessness that I want so desperately to kiss away.

Leaning forward, I press my lips against his urging him on. He runs his tongue across my bottom lip; I let out a gasp and his tongue enters, tasting every inch of me. Clint's hand cradles my ass, lifting me effortlessly. My legs wrap around his waist.

I can feel his pulse rapidly beating as I kiss up his neck. It's beating as fast as my own. "I need to feel you inside me."

He does not hesitate. Bracing me against the door, he lets go of my ass and pulls his shirt over his head before attacking my top and freeing me of my bra. I rake my lips across his bare shoulders and up his neck tasting his salty sweat. He carries me away from the door, heading for the kitchen. Gingerly, he lays me down on the counter. It's cold, sending shivers down my spine, but I ignore it. Soon, Clint will heat my body.

"I have wanted to lay you out like this since I met you," he pants. Tugging on my jeans, he tears the last of my clothes off. "I want to feast off of you."

Grabbing hold of my hips, Clint leans down. Drawing my budded nipple into his mouth while palming my other breast, he ignites those tingles only his touch can spark. Slowly, he kisses across my chest and sucks in my other nipple, paying equal attention to it. He slides down my body, raining down tender yet urgent kisses. He makes his way to the junction of my legs. "You're soaked," he groans when his mouth grazes over my clit. He slides in one of his massive fingers.

I buck hard against his face. His other hand pushes down on my stomach, holding me down right where he wants me. My whole-body quakes as his tongue dives deeper into my folds. Another finger slides in, stretching me. I can't stop grinding harder on his hand. I feel the orgasm building up inside me. It is ready to rip through me. I tighten my lower abdomen. He sucks hard on my clit, driving me insane. I lose all control, screaming his name as I shatter to a million pieces.

Opening my eyes, Clint watches me, spellbound. His pupils are dilated almost black. "You're my everything." He says, his voice straining with every word as his fingers slide slowly out of me. Clenching tight on his fingers, I want to hold on to them longer, but he pulls them from me and brings them to his lips, sucking them dry. "You taste so sweet."

We stare deep into each other's eyes while he takes his boots and jeans off. There is so much love and desire in my gentle giant. He looks vulnerable and it breaks my heart. Standing there for a moment, he lets me admire him before he steps between my legs. Lining himself up he nudges my entrance.

"I love you," he whispers, sounding disquieted.

"I love you," I say, and I make a wish we won't lose each other when this is all over.

Sliding in slowly, Clint lets me stretch around him. He pulls out slowly before thrusting deeper. I arch my back and curl my toes. The man feels incredible. His hands grab my hips while he thrusts deeper. There is something carnal about our lovemaking on his counter. My abdomen tightens as my orgasm builds. Gliding his hands up my sides, he lifts my arms above my head pinning them to the countertop with one of his hands. I am stretched out tight taking every demanding thrust. Wanting more, I can't get enough of him. His lips hover just above mine. His warm breath tickles my skin and it smells like cinnamon. Lifting my head, I try to kiss him, but he pulls away.

"Tell me what you want?" he asks, denying my second attempt to kiss him.

"To kiss you," I breath out as my climbing orgasm strangles my voice.

"No, tell me what you *really* want," he says. His free hand tickles my side and he doesn't slow his pace. "Tell me," he growls. Thrusting hard, he hits the spot that turns my orgasm into a tidal wave of emotion crashing into my heart over and over, before it sweeps me into its current, drowning me in extasy.

"Tell me," he pants again.

I can feel him close to letting go. "A future. A future with you," I admit, breathing hard. My heart still racing from the earth-shattering orgasm.

Clint sucks in a breath. Letting out a growl, he picks up the pace. Pounding into me again and again before roaring as he lets go deep inside me.

"I want forever," he says between breaths, laying his forehead against my chest. He releases my hands. "Tell me you want forever."

I wrap my arms around his neck. "I want forever with you."

25

- Clint -

I'm playing with fire by not using protection. The first time, I truly wasn't in the right mind. So, wrapped up in Dawn. Wanting nothing more than to make love to her, all I could think about was being inside her. I know I shouldn't have done what I wanted to, feeling her from the inside with no constraints. Feel what is mine and bury myself so deep there is no return. It's not the time to bring a baby into the world, but I'm risking it. I don't even know if she wants kids.

"Do you want kids?" I blurt out, not thinking. I'm still reeling from the single most life altering orgasm.

"Yes," she says, watching me carefully. "I want a little girl someday."

I pull out of her, but don't let her go. Instead I carry her to our bedroom and lay her on our bed. I'll never be able to look at the counter again without the images of her beautiful body laid out on it. Still watching me carefully, she flushes as her cheeks redden and her blonde hair tumbles around her shoulders. She's stunning.

"You look like you have bad news," she says, a worried look wipes away the satisfied smile I had just put on her face.

Amanda Lee Dixon

"I haven't been using any protection," I confess, watching her eyes grow wide. I could punch myself. I hate seeing fear and sadness cross her perfect face. I'd lay down my life if it meant putting a permeant smile on her face. I never believed in love stories that defied everything. I always thought they were fairytales until Dawn came into my life. Now I know what all the fuss is about. Why grown men lose their mind.

"Oh," she squeaks out, looking more frighten.

I won't lie; frightening her stings. "Are you mad?" I ask, hoping I don't have to pry her thoughts out. If I'm being honest, some primal force in me secretly wants her to be mine forever, and planting my seed is one way of doing it, but she deserved to have a say. I shouldn't have taken that away from her.

"I don't know what to say."

"Say you aren't mad," I throw out. If she isn't mad at me for being territorial and controlling, I can forgive myself.

"I'm not mad," she says looking at her stomach. "Worried."

"Having a baby right now isn't ideal," I admit, scratching the back of my head. I manage a small smile when she looks up at me, I can't read hear expression. She looks conflicted.

"Do you want kids?" She's still holding her stomach, and maybe I feel a little relieved. Maybe she isn't worried about getting pregnant even during this shit storm we're in. The way her eyes search mine, a twinkle of excite reflect back at me, igniting a flame that starts in my chest, spreading downward into a throb, stirring my cock back to life. I need to be inside her again.

"As many as you will give me," I answer, kissing her lips softly. I can feel her smile.

"I'd like to be married first," she breathes into my mouth sounding uncertain, and that throb turns to a consuming need to make her mine, not just physically but biblically.

"Oh, I'm going to marry you," I bite her lip, not letting her respond. She moans opening her mouth.

Invitation received, my tongue slides in slowly. I need her to feel my love in this kiss. To know exactly what forever with me feels like. I want this kiss to be the kiss that seals our fate together, seals her heart, body and soul with me forever.

Lifting her up her legs wrap around my waist my cock roaring to be inside her. She drives me wild: her taste, her smell, her soft silky skin, those bewitching eyes. It's like a madness that takes over and my only cure is her.

"Let's take a shower before work," I suggest, leading her towards the bathroom where we wash, touch, and explore each other's body until the water runs cold.

*****

Later that night at closing, I helped Dawn put the last of the chairs onto the tables. "Sarah and Eric said they were coming by Benny's, right?" Dawn asks, sounding concerned. Earlier today, Eric called to say Sarah and him would stop by before closing to talk through some details before he took Sarah back to her hotel. However, Dawn closed the bar down thirty minutes ago and still no sign of Eric or Sarah since they took off.

"Eric's phone is going directly to voicemail. Sarah isn't answering." I've called six times only his phone goes straight to voicemail. "If they are fucking in my bed, I'll kill him!"

"Do you think they are at your apartment?" She asks lifting an eyebrow at me with a smirk.

Eric and Sarah are clearly attracted to each other, and they both are probably too proud and too stubborn to admit it. I doubt neither of them will make the first move. "Hopefully," I mutter, not liking their absence. It's not like Eric to not call or text if things change. If anything, he's OCD about schedules.

"Should we call Benny? Maybe Sarah is with her parent's and lost track of time."

"If they aren't at my apartment, we can call Benny," I offer. Eric and Sarah not showing up can only mean one thing. I pity anyone who tries to mess with my brother. He's a force to be reckoned with. Hell, all us Colson men are, but we aren't invincible and if Sal or the Port Pirates are trying to get to Dawn, it makes sense for them to go after Eric and Sarah first.

Dawn grabs her coat from the closet. I help her put it on before leading her out the door to lock up. The chilly air smacks me in the face. I glance around, looking for any sign of trouble. There are no cars in the parking lot or surrounding area, and Eric's car isn't parked at my apartment across the street. The hairs on the back of my neck rise. I don't want Dawn to pick up on how jumpy I am, but something isn't right. I feel it in my bones and given everything that has happened I should be paying attention to my gut.

"Well, if it isn't the two love birds," Sal's familiar voice sings out. He creeps slowly around the corner of Benny's Bar. His smug smile nearly has me lunging at him but the pistol he points at us puts my brakes on. "I see you called your lawyer friend. She's a beauty. Shame she couldn't be here to play. I had hoped to get a taste of her."

"Oh, God," Dawn cries out.

I push her behind me, even with a gun pointed at me I will protect her. This guy is sick, and I will be damned if I let him live, even if I have to kill him with my bare hands. "What did you do to them?" I ask, forcing myself to sound calm. If I can stall Sal long enough, I might figure a way out of this. Side stepping around us Sal cuts off any opportunity to run and pinning us against Benny's Bar.

"They had some car trouble," he sneers, his yellowing teeth on full display. "Now as much as I would love to play, I've got a client who wants his property."

"Your client can go fuck himself!" I growl, pressing Dawn tight into my back. I can hear her little hiccups, each one flaring my anger. We are exactly where she didn't want to be, but I couldn't let her run. Even if it means our time together is about to end.

"Who is your client?" an unfamiliar voice from the left of us asks, I nearly give myself whip lash. The stranger emerges from the dark shadows by the corner Sal came around. Coming out of the shadows, the man is tall but even in the soft glow from the front light his features are blurry. Relief relaxes my shoulders when I see him point his gun at Sal.

Dawn gasps, as she peeks around my shoulder. My stomach drops noticing the leather vest he is wearing, I have no doubt has Port Pirates on the back, this must be Darin. Gripping her tighter, I snarl at the man responsible for the terror Dawn has in her eyes.

"I had hoped you were dead in the woods," Sal sneers, looking giddy at the stranger, but keeps his gun pointed at us.

"You have shitty aim. You ok, Dawn?" The stranger asks, chancing a glance at her.

A jealousy I've never felt before claws at my belly along with the urge to pummel the man who is responsible for all of Dawn's fears. I want to rip his limbs off but first I need to get Dawn somewhere safe.

"She's fine," I growl, turning us, so neither man can see her tucked close behind me. Dawn's breathing picks up. How I can get her away safely from them both without getting shot in the process? Scanning the area there isn't much coverage. Really the only option is to push her toward the end of the building and make a run for it. With the cover of night both men would be shooting blind.

"Looks like your girl found someone else to warm her bed," Sal taunts Darin who barely glances at me. If we are lucky, and luck really isn't on my side, the two will keep each other occupied long enough for me to get Dawn away safely.

"Looks like you're still doing Harvey's dirty work." Darin retorts with a shrug. "He never liked getting his hands dirty."

"Shut up!" Sal spits, turning his gun toward Darin. That struck a chord. I use the opportunity to sidestep towards the corner of Benny's Bar.

"I always knew you were his bitch, but I never thought you had the chops," Darin laughs, taking a step forward.

I take another step. Dawn tumbles behind me but my hold on her helps her stay upright.

"Don't you fucking move!" Sal screams at me, pointing the gun. "And you," he swings the gun back towards Darin, "you come any closer, I'll shoot the girl."

"She has nothing to do with the beef we have."

"I know that!" Sal returns, not taking his eyes off Darin who looks worried. "I needed her to pull you out of whatever gutter you were hiding in."

Darin moves in again. Sal points the gun at Darin and I move too, faster towards safety. Sal aims his gun back toward my chest. By the way he switches his aim on Darin and I, Sal is getting desperate, and desperation is dangerous.

A gunshot rings out into the chilly air, and I jerk back into Dawn. Fire bursting from Sal's barrel, another follows as he shoots at me. Were they warning shots? Sal turns to point the gun on Darin before a blinding pain tears through my bicep. Stunned, I sag back more pinning Dawn against the wall. I don't know why I touch my shoulder; my actions don't seem to be my own. My hand is wet. I look at it and the red liquid seems foreign. Is this my blood? I know I should care about it, but I'm too dazed or shock to be concerned.

I think Dawn is screaming, but the pounding in my head drowns her out. Slumping down the wall, I watch Darin and Sal point their guns at each other. I turn my head up to see Dawn. Those beautiful fearful eyes glisten with tears. She's trying to tell me something. Why is she talking to me? She needs to run. Adrenaline pumps through my veins, keeping me coherent, but my limbs aren't working the way I need them to. I choke out for her to run before my legs give out from under me.

Another shot rings out. I scream, "Run!" It comes out more clearly this time. I push her with the last of my energy. My shoulder feels like it's on fire, and my adrenaline does nothing to cloak it. Staring into Dawn's fearful eyes, I know she's trying to tell me something important, but I can't concentrate. Her beautiful lips are moving. They look so soft I want to taste them, but she has to get out of here. I try to push her again only to fall to my side. She tries to hold me up, staggering under my weight, but gives up and somehow manages to lay me flat on my back. Distantly, I feel her putting pressure on my shoulder. I try to brush her away, the pain is white hot. Why isn't she running?

A dizziness has everything spinning around me, I try to zero in on Dawn. My beautiful Sweetness hovers above me, saying something in a mute language. Why are we in slow motion? Everything dims when Darin stands over me, his hand on Dawn's shoulder. He stares down at me, looking grim. My vision swims before me. I fight to get up, screaming at him, but the darkness consumes me and spirals me into a shadowy nothing.

26

- Dawn -

"Don't close your eyes Clint! You have to stay awake!" I yell at him. He looks so pale. Blood is pooling on to the ground. "Please, just open your eyes!"

"Dawn…" Someone tugs at me while I cling to Clint. I need to keep pressure on his wounds. So much blood. I have to stop the bleeding.

"No!" I cry, pulling out of his grasp. "I'm not leaving him!"

"Babe, we've got to go," the familiar voice says into my ear. His arms wrap around my waist lifting me up off the ground.

Throwing back my head, I buck against the solid chest I'm pinned to. "No!" I scream, thrashing harder. "Let me go!"

"I can't leave you here. Not like this," the man who has haunted my dreams says. "We have to get out of here."

"Please, he will die! Let me help him," I beg. I'm growing weak as the struggle wears me out. I can hear the defeat in my voice, "Please!"

"The cops will be here soon. He'll be fine." Darin's breath on my neck makes me cringe. He's still alive.

"I can't leave him," I hiccup, sounding so broken. I watch the distance grow between Clint and me. "Please!"

"Babe, you aren't safe anymore. I've got to get you out of here," he whispers in my ear. Sirens sing far away, and I pause my thrashing in relief. Darin takes my stillness as submission and quickens his pace.

"Not safe?" You are the reason I'm not safe!" I scream at him, clawing at his arms around me. Darin has always been strong, working at the docks kept him in shape. I'm useless against him, but still I push, pull, and scratch, hoping it will loosen his hold on me enough to escape.

"I didn't think Harvey and Sal would go after you." Darin tries to justify, pulling me further and further away from Clint. "Sorry."

"*Sorry*! You're *sorry*?" I growl as my fists pound against his arms with no effect. "I thought you were dead! I filed a missing person report. I have almost been killed twice now. The man I love maybe dying and all you have to say is *sorry*!"

"Love?" Darin asks pulling me in front of Clint's salvage yard tucked behind his Auto Body Shop.

"Yes, love!" I yell moving on to using my legs to try and kick his. Anything to get free from the iron grip that encases me against Darin's chest. "Did you think I would wait for you?"

"Not this soon." He admits pulling on the padlock on the sliding fence door to the salvage yard. It pops open as if it wasn't even locked, and I wonder if he had picked it prior to showing up to Benny's.

"It's been two years!" I stomp on his foot, but it does nothing against his combat boots. The sirens are getting closer. I glance over Darin's shoulder to where Clint and Sal lay outside of Benny's Bar. I should be with Clint. "Please let me go."

"We need to get out of here. The cops will swarm this whole area soon."

"I'm not going anywhere with you." I grunt as I lift my legs to brace against the fencing preventing Darin from moving us forward through the opening.

"Stop being so difficult!" He hisses pulling us away from the opening, turning around and walking backward through the gate. Tears burn my eyes. My throat feels swollen from screaming. I hate this feeling of hopelessness. For two years, I have lived without hope, until Clint somehow changed that, and now he is laying in a pool of his own blood, and it's all my fault. I brought this ugly mess into his life. All my fault. All my fault. Silently I cry in defeat whisper my fault while Darin carries me through the salvage yard. The streetlights barely shine past the fencing as we drift further in, in almost complete darkness.

Darin loosens his grip, and I try to free myself from him, but the effort is futile.

"My bike's outside the back fencing. We can slip out before the cops search the area."

"I told you I'm not going with you." I say with less intensity. I'm so exhausted and defeated.

"Dawn I killed a man. We can't stay here." Darin sighs as if he's talking to a child. What did I ever see in this man?

"Then you leave." I retort.

The sirens are louder now. They must have arrived.

"Keep your voice down, don't make any sounds." Darin whispers into my ear. Faint red and blue lights dance off the towering cars.

"And if I don't?" Every part of me wants to scream but I know Darin. He's stubborn, and used to getting what he wants. If I have any chance of getting away its by convincing him to let me go.

"Dawn don't do this." Darin sighs with frustration.

"Fine, but you have to tell me what happened to you. Why you left. You owe me that." I say aiming to appeal to the side of Darin I think may still care for me.

"We don't have time to play catch up." Darin groans but slows his pace.

"You've been gone for two years. You can't expect me to just run off with you. Not after what you've put me through." I force my body to relax against him. Apply some guilt and let him think I won't fight anymore. I hate playing games and being manipulative, but I will play dirty and be convincing if it means getting to Clint.

"If I let you go will you promise not to run?"

"I promise." I whisper putting a little tenderness in my voice. There once was a time when Darin use to ask me to promise him all kinds of things. Nothing impossible just little things. He loved it when I made promises to him and kept those promises. He would tell me I was the only person he knew that could keep a promise.

Darin's nose subtly trails up my neck, breathing in my scent. It takes all my control not to flinch. His touch has become foreign to me and feels so wrong. He's not Clint.

Darin releases me but doesn't step away. I turn to face him, forcing myself to stay close to him. The darkness masks his features. His hand comes up to brush against my cheek. I don't want this, but I have to convince him to let me go.

"Why did you leave?"

"Billy and I were working a job with Harvey and Sal. Harvey needed us as muscle while he worked a deal with some thugs Sal hooked him up with. I didn't know much about the job, they instructed us to monitor the men that showed up at the meeting spot." Darin explains, his hand moving from my cheek to my shoulder, he holds a piece of my hair in his hands. It was something he used to do, when we were together. "The goods Harvey was buying I now know were drugs. The Port Pirates don't deal in drugs, so it was something he and Sal were doing rogue. During the exchange Sal opened fire, so Billy and I did as well. After the thugs went down Sal turned on us. He killed Billy, but we both shot at him, we were

271

too shocked at Sal turning on us our aim wasn't worth shit. I took cover close to the money Harvey brought. I open fired, grabbed the money and took off. Sal got a few shots off and one hit me in the back."

Darin pauses, his hand continues to slides down my arm, taking my hand in his. Clint's blood is still on my hands, my clothes. Bile climbs my throat as I try to fight the desperate need to yank my hand from his.

"I wanted to come for you, but I thought it was safer to leave you alone. Cut any communication to you so they would think I was dead. I called a buddy of mine, an ex-military medic. He patched me up and let me lie low in his cousin's cabin."

"John? You called John?" I ask remembering Darin's friend John who was honorably discharged from the military. "He came to my apartment to see how I was doing. He never told you about what the Port Pirates were doing to me?"

"He told me." Darin drops his head looking guilty. "He said it was harmless shit that was aimed to scare you into telling them where I was. Since you didn't know I figured they would let up."

"Well, they didn't," I reply pulling my hand from his and crossing my arms around myself. "Why didn't you go to a hospital or call the police?"

The sirens are fading. The blue and red still flash faintly and I hope the sirens are from an ambulance taking Clint to a hospital. If the sirens are on, he must be alive. I cling to that hope as Darin puts his hands on my shoulders and squeezes. Turning me he pushes me down the dark path towards the back of the salvage yard.

"We have to leave now. No more talking."

"Darin why didn't you go the police?" I stop walking and turn to face him again. Stalling tactic I pray will buy me time so the police can come search the area.

"Because I couldn't rat against my MC." He hisses running his hands through his hair. "I had to figure out what Harvey and Sal were up to. If I could put a stop to them, I knew I could fall back into the Port Pirates good graces."

"Just like that, and everything would be back to normal." I cross my arms again trying not to think about the wetness in my clothes from Clint's blood. "All that time we were together I thought you were working at the docks, but really you were pulling jobs for the Port Pirates."

"I worked at the docks. I needed a job, or it would have made me and the MC look suspicious."

"I'm such an idiot." I whisper, bitterness coating my tongue. How did I not know this? Were there signs that I missed? "I was such a fool. Were you ever going to tell me?"

"You're not an idiot or a fool." Darin takes a step closer, but I step away. Even through the darkness I know that stung him. "I was going to tell you."

"Before or after you finally got caught?" I counter taking another step away from him.

"Dawn…"

"What's your plan now?" I cut him off.

"I have enough evidence to bring Harvey down." Darin says but stiffens when a noise comes from behind us. "We've got to leave now."

"So, you can go back to your Port Pirates?" I ask sounding outraged, but he ignores my question and grabs my wrists and pulls me into his chest. "I'm done running Darin. The police will know I was with Clint. They will look for me."

"I can get you a new identity. I can keep you hidden." He hisses into my ear turning me around and pushing me forward.

"I don't want to go with you. That life ended the second you left me behind." I say grounding my heels into the dirt, but it does little to stop Darin from moving me forward. In one quick swoop he lifts me up, throwing me over his shoulder and continues his march as if I weigh nothing. As if my protests mean nothing.

"I'm sorry I left you. I should've had John come get you and bring you to me, but you were happy. You finally had a permeant home. You would've been miserable having to move around again." Darin justifies while he marches on.

I can't fight Darin while over his shoulder. He's too strong, but there is no way he can keep a hold of me while on his bike, so I stay quiet and let him carry me. I strain my ears for sounds of approaching police officers, but all I hear is silence. Are they even thinking of looking here? The trek to Darin's bike doesn't take long and soon he is setting me down.

"I'm not going back." I state while I try to not wobble on my feet as the blood rushes back down my body. Darin helps steady me, but I step out of his reach.

"We could start over." Darin suggestions softly, I can hear the doubt in his voice, feel his eyes on me, waiting for me to give in. Instead, I focus on his doubt.

"My whole adolescent life was filled with disappointment, one after the other. Always being let down until I had no more hope. Then I met you." I relax my body as I take a step closer to him so he can really see me. "You never let me down, never disappointed me."

"Dawn I promise never to disappoint you again. I'm so damn sorry." Darin's hands wrap around my face pulling me close, he leans in close and I can feel his breath on my face.

"But you are disappointing me." I whisper, Darin's lips brush against mine. "Let me go."

Darin swallows, pulling back slightly. "If I let you go, you have to go on the run. The Port Pirates and the police will be after us both."

"Deep down I think I always knew you never loved me as much as I loved you." I admit to myself more than to Darin. Maybe I was so tired of being disappointed and never loved unconditionally like my mother had loved me I allowed myself to settle. I'm sure the signs were all there I just ignored them.

"You were my everything! I loved you!" Darin snaps and smashes his mouth against mine. It's a desperate, brutal kiss that I don't return. A cold anger seeps into my pores and chills my bones. I push away from him.

"If you truly love me you would turn yourself in." I spit, whipping my mouth.

"I killed a man Dawn. You want to see me locked up?" Darin quips then steps around me toward the fence. "I'm better off on the run."

"Then you only prove to be my biggest disappointment." I say turning to watch him remove several fence boards, the nails holding them all pried off. "Talk to my friend Sarah. She can help you. You shot Sal out of self-defense."

"What is she a lawyer or something?"

"Yes, and if you have evidence against Harvey maybe you can work out a deal?" I say walking over to where he stands by the fence opening.

"I can't rat on the Port Pirates." He says pinching the bridge of his nose. "I'm not a rat Dawn."

"Think about it?"

"Just promise me you don't hate me." Darin says and steps through the fence opening, I can just make out his motorcycle close to where he stands.

"One condition." I step through the fence opening.

"What's that?" He crosses his arms eyeing me suspiciously.

"Promise me you will take me to the hospital."

He says nothing and I think I may have asked for too much. "Fine," He nods then walks to his motorcycle where he helps me on. Darin puts his helmet on me then climbs on before peering over his shoulder and says "You have to say it. Promise me you don't hate me."

"I don't hate you."

*****

"Dawn!" Amber's voice cries out as I enter the ER area. Luke is standing next to her. His face looks grim. "You're covered in blood."

"It's not mine. How his Clint?" I ask as she pulls me into a hug. She hugs me tight and I'm so tired I'm not ashamed to want to stay in her arms.

"He's stable, they are operating on him now." Amber shares and relief floods through me. All I want to do is be with Clint and maybe then melt into the hospital floor and sleep for a week.

"The police are looking for you. They think you killed the man they found with Clint." Luke asks and to my surprise pulls me into a hug. A hug I picture a brother would give to a sister and it calms some anxiety that has been building since Clint and I closed Benny's.

"I didn't kill him. Darin did." I reveal when Luke releases me. "I need to find Sarah and Eric. Do you guys know what happened to them?"

"They're here. Eric brought Sarah here about an hour before Clint was brought in." Amber shares and then grabs my hand, "I'll take you too her. She's in exam bed one, waiting for a CT scan."

"Are they ok?" I ask not sure if I should weep or be relieved. Sal was so vague in what happened to them. Guilt churns my stomach. I have brought nothing but trouble to everyone who has done nothing but kind things for me. I honestly don't understand how any of them could possibly be worried about me when it is all my fault they are hurting.

"Eric is banged up but fine. Sarah hit her head hard in the car accident and has a broken arm, but nothing serious." Amber tells me as she leads me past the nurse's station toward the exam beds. Luke is following us.

"This is all my fault." I mutter more to myself. I'm not sure I want to face Sarah, especially Eric. From the moment Clint called him he has wanted me far away from Clint.

"None of this is your fault." Luke says putting a hand on my shoulder before I can walk around the exam room curtain. "Eric filled me in on everything. You didn't ask for this and what happened to Clint isn't your fault. Don't beat yourself up over it. He will need you when he gets out of surgery and you need to stay strong for him."

I don't know what to say to that so I only nod at him as my eyes fill up with tears. Looking over at Amber she seems equally shocked by Luke's words. Luke only shrugs when he notices Amber eyeing him.

"Let's get in to see Sarah. The Sheriff is somewhere around here waiting to speak with Clint, and I don't want him catching you before you've talked with Sarah." Luke nudges us to move around the exam bed curtain.

"Dawn! Oh, thank God." Sarah cries out as we walk in. She makes to get out of bed, but Eric stops her.

"Both of you sit." Eric orders and I happily comply taking a seat in the chair next to Sarah's bed.

"We've been so worried." Sarah says shooting Eric a glare, but she doesn't leave her bed. Both her and Eric are covered in superficial cuts and scrapes. Eric has a larger gash across his left cheek and dark circles under his eyes. There is a worried almost frantic expression on his face I suspect is because of Sarah's injuries. Sarah has a big knot above her swollen right eye that has already turned a painful purple and maroon. Her arm is in a temporary splint that she keeps elevated on a pillow.

"Are you guys ok?" I tentatively ask. Despite Luke's reassurance that none of this is my fault, seeing both Eric and Sarah's injuries make it hard to believe him.

"We are fine, and from what I hear Clint will be fine so don't you dare start blaming yourself." Sarah says with her best pointed stare though her swollen eye makes it look more like a grimace.

"Sal cut our brake fluid." Eric alleges, his jaw is tense and there is a deep seeded fury he isn't keeping well concealed.

"Eric managed to slow us down some, but Sal tried to run us off the road and we rolled the vehicle." Sarah finishes grabbing Eric's hand and giving it a squeeze. "Eric's phone was crushed in the wreck and he couldn't find mine. I blacked out and he carried me to the road and flagged down a passing car."

"Sal must have gone straight to Benny's after he ran you guys off the road. He was waiting for us when we locked up." I add, flashes of Clint being shot replay in my head.

"Who shot Sal?" Eric asks and I push away the nightmarish memories.

"Darin." I say and retell them all everything. I walk them through every horrifying detail, answer all of Eric and Sarah's questions until my voice goes horse and Amber stops them and forces me to drink some water.

"We should have someone look you over. You may be in shock from the trauma." Amber suggestions as she refills my water cup.

"So, he's gone?" Luke asks where he stands by his brother Eric.

"I gave him Sarah's number and told him to call you, but I don't think he will rat on the Port Pirates. It will get him killed." I answer looking to Sarah. "Now what?"

"We talk to the Sheriff." Sarah replies with a grimace. "He will want to question you and may still consider you a suspect in Sal's shooting. At least until Clint wakes up and he can witness to Darin's resurfacing."

"Will I be arrested?" I sound so small. I'm so tired and exhausted, being arrested and interrogated for hours only sounds more torturous.

"Doubtful, besides I will be with you for all the questioning." Sarah assures then looks to Amber. "Do you think you can admit Dawn and have her looked over?"

"I'm fine…"

"You need to be looked over and you need rest." Sarah cuts me off. "This will also buy us some time. If Clint gets out of surgery and provides a witness statement before you are released, he won't have a reason to arrest you."

"I'll get started on getting her admitted." Amber says and leaves. "Luke you want to come with me and get an update on Clint?"

"Sure." Luke says sounding a little shocked but can't stop his cocky grin from spreading wide across his face.

"Don't read into it." Amber glares then disappears behind the curtain with Luke trailing close behind her.

"The Port Pirates will find out about what happened. They'll know where to find me." I state the obvious to Sarah and Eric once Luke and Amber are out of hearing range. "I'm putting everyone in danger all over again."

"The Port Pirates will finally know for sure Darin is alive and with Sal out of the picture they will probably look for Darin now." Eric responds with narrowed eyes. "Are you thinking about running?"

"No. I promised Clint I wouldn't, but I can't help but think staying will only bring more trouble to everyone. I don't want to see everyone I care about suffer anymore." I confess rubbing my temples.

"Why don't you let me worry about everyone's safety and you focus on nursing Clint back to health." Eric suggests crossing his arms over his chest, his icy blue eyes so much like Clint's it hurts to look at him.

Looking away from those familiar eyes I nod my agreement. Everything feels too easy, too convenient and almost too good to be true.

"It will be hard for a while, but we're all here to help." Sarah chimes in with a sympathetic smile. She always knew how to sooth away some of my darkest thoughts. "It may even suck for a while, but you will get through this, with all of us by your side."

"Clint is out of surgery and in stable condition. He's in post-op but the Sheriff won't let anyone see him until he questions him," Amber shares as she comes around the curtain. She goes to the other side of the exam bed and pulls the curtain back revealing an empty bed. "Hop in Dawn, this is your exam bed. We need to pull some blood and take your vitals."

"Let's finally get this over with." I stand and head for the exam bed.

"At least you won't be alone in here." Sarah smiles at me, and I can't help but smile back even if it takes the last of my strength.

27

- Clint -

"He just left?" I ask Eric unsure how I feel about Darin's disappearing act. At least he didn't take Dawn with him. The scumbag deserves whatever comes his way even if he stopped Sal from pursuing Dawn.

It's been three days since Sal shot me. One hit my arm, but it was just a flesh wound. The other into my shoulder that required surgery to pull the slug out and stop the bleeding. Luckily no major organs and blood vessels were hit.

"Yeah. Sheriff McKnight has put out an APB, but this is a man whose been living off the grid for two years. He's probably using an alias." Eric shares, looking steely as he snatches my Jell-O cup off my bedside table. "It's the kind of challenge I'm looking forward to tackling."

"You're going after Darin?" I ask in disbelief. I honestly expected Eric to be halfway back to Texas by now, but I am glad he stuck around. I'll never admit it but I like having him around. I've missed his cranky ass.

"Catching Darin before Sheriff McKnight only sweetens the pot." Eric smirks before shoving a spoonful of Jell-O into his mouth. "McKnight is a bigger asshole than his dad."

"He's an asshole because Jax was notorious for making his dad look like a fool." I point out, but Eric is right. Sheriff McKnight is an asshole with a giant chip on his shoulder when it comes to us Colson men. At least he wasn't too hard on Dawn while questioning her, though Sarah had something to do with that I suspect.

"Dawn said they are releasing you tomorrow." Eric comments finishing up my Jell-O and tossing it into the wastebasket. "She's coming with lunch, right?"

"Yeah she said she'd be up here by now." I furrow my brow, checking the time. "Do you think the Port Pirates will come looking for her?"

"No, but Harvey the MC President has some connections that concern me. Don't worry I have eyes on him. He can't sneeze without me knowing about it." He reveals pulling his phone from his pocket and scrolling through something on the screen. "Besides, I think Harvey will focus on Darin."

"Do you think Darin will come back?"

"I'll likely find him before he does." Eric smiles a cocky smile that is a lot like Luke's. "Yes, I'm that good."

"You're as arrogant as Luke." I mutter not feeling convinced Dawn is truly safe from the Port Pirates.

"Are you worried Dawn will leave your sorry ass for him?"

"No," I glare at my annoying brother.

"Good. I've seen the way she looks at you. Like you hung the damn moon." He chuckles with a wink before picking up the remote and flipping through the TV channels.

"Sarah looks at you like that." I give him a pointed stare and a ghost of a smile appears on his stone-cold face.

"Nah, she's just excited everything is working out." He deflects, then settles on some crime show documentary. "She lives halfway across the country."

"Boy, what are you still doing in that hospital bed?" Burns' booming voice interrupts as he walks into my hospital room. "Rub some dirt on it."

"Old man you always know when to pop in when you aren't welcome." I hurl back but shake his hand with my good one when he steps up to my bed. I see him eyeing me, checking to make sure I'm ok. I know deep down the man is worried but hiding it knowing we would make a big deal about his fussing.

"Miss Janet made you a get well soon cherry pie, but I ate it before I made it up here." Burns says while walking around the bed to shake Eric's hand and then steal his seat. It's the only recliner in the room and the most comfortable seat.

"Never change Burns." Eric laughs and takes up a seat next to my bed.

"I suppose you're about to take off without so much as a goodbye." Burns grunts picking up the remote and flipping through the channels.

"It is my style." Eric admits patting the old man on the shoulder. His smile not quite reaching his eyes. I wonder if Sarah might be the reason, he's sticking around longer than expected.

"Where's Dawn?" Burns asking pausing on a show that looks a lot like a soap opera.

"She should be here." I glance at the clock worry tickling my stomach. First thing I intend to do is get her a damn cell phone that I can low jack.

"Good, I heard she was bringing up lunch and I'm starving." Burns says patting his belly.

"Don't you have a girlfriend to cook for you?" Eric remarks still fiddling with his phone.

"Yes, but I want second lunch." Burns says matter-of-factly and turns up the volume on the TV.

"He's bossier than I remember." Eric whispers settling in his chair and putting his phone away.

"I heard that." Burns snaps and turns the volume up even more. "Miss Janet loves her stories and got me hooked on this one."

"Well doesn't this look like a sorry lot of yuppies." Luke greets with that cocky grin from the door.

"Who you calling a yuppy?" Burns growls not taking his eyes off the TV. "You jackwagon!"

"Where's Dawn?" Luke asks pulling a chair up next to Eric.

"I'm doing well, thanks for asking." I roll my eyes before glancing at the clock again.

"I heard she was bringing up lunch." Luke says tilting his head in question at the TV. "What is this?"

"One of Miss Janet's favorite stories, now shut it jackwagon." Burns quips and turns the volume up more. It's blaring as the sounds of his story plays. "This is the part where Clementine's dead husband Augustine returns after being lost at sea."

"Can you turn it down?" Luke shouts over the sounds of a damsel in distress after seeing her lost dead but really alive husband.

"Only if you zip it jackwagon." Burns says and turns the volume down a little.

"So, are we rooting for this Augustine guy?" Luke smirks sending me a wink and a mischievous smile.

"Do not engage." Eric smacks Luke upside the head.

"Touch me again and you lose a hand you jackwagon." Luke punches Eric who shoves him.

"Boys, enough!" Amber claps her hands from the door before entering. "I'll have security throw you both out."

"Throw them out!" Burns waves but continues to be engrossed in his stories.

"How are you feeling?" Amber asks coming to my bedside and leaning over for a hug and a quick peck on the cheek. She feels my forehead and checks on my chart.

"I feel good, ready to be home."

"Looks like they plan to let you loose tomorrow." Amber notes before putting the chart back and taking a seat on the end of the bed. "Where's Dawn?"

"Not here." I roll my eyes. Does everyone want her food? Who am I kidding of course they do. She's a phenomenal cook, but I'm still not admitting that to her. I love riling her up. She's so adorable when she gets heated.

"Sorry I'm late," Dawn says as she walks through the door carrying a large crock pot and a bag of disposable bowls and spoons.

"Finally!" Burns says jumping up from his chair. "Ay! Jackwagons, help the poor girl!"

"Yeah, you jackwagons!" I chime in as my nerves calm seeing Dawn safe and sound. Worry will be my constant companion when Dawn isn't by my side. At least not until Darin and the Port Pirates cease to exist.

"Where's Sarah I thought she was coming with you?" Eric asks taking the crock pot and bag from Dawn and setting on the back counter. Everyone swarms in, unpacking the bowls and spoons and ladles out the soup.

The smell of clams hits me and my stomach grumbles with hunger. Dawn comes over to my bed-side table looking a little tired and pale.

"Sarah is on her way." Dawn says before leaning in and giving me a kiss. Something isn't right, she seems off. I scan her from head to toe but can't quite pinpoint what's different about her.

"Here yuppy I got you a bowl of clam chowder before the jackwagons ate it all." Burns brings over a bowl of steaming chowder that makes my mouth water. "It smells delicious *Sweetness*!"

"Watch it old man. She's mine," I glare at him taking the bowl from Burns.

"I think I'm going to be sick." Dawn rushes for the bathroom that is to the left of my bed. Everyone stops what they are doing watching the closed bathroom door.

"Is she ok?" Burns asks looking at me as sounds of Dawn getting sick comes through the door.

"Dawn you ok?" Amber calls through the bathroom door, then scoops in a bite of her chowder.

Dawn mumbles something incoherent, before more vomit sounds follow.

"I hope you guys didn't eat all the clam chowder." Sarah calls out from the room entrance before zeroing in on the clam chowder. "What did I miss?"

"Dawn's sick," Eric whispers to Sarah as the toilet flushes. "I wouldn't eat that."

"Oh, I bet it's just morning sickness," Sarah shrugs and ladles out some chowder.

"Morning sickness?" Everyone including myself questions. That can only mean one thing.

"Oh no," Sarah mumbles with chowder in her mouth. "She hasn't told you?"

"She's pregnant?" I ask looking at the closed bathroom door as it opens, and a slightly flushed Dawn emerges. "You're pregnant?"

"Um…" She lifts her shoulders and winces before looking at everyone. "I was going to tell you when we got home."

"Sorry Dawn," Sarah whispers then shoves a spoonful of chowder in her mouth, her face red with embarrassment.

"Come here," I wave her over.

Her cheeks flush, and she bites her lip, something she does when she's nervous.

"Dr. Cantana told me when they released me from the hospital," she reveals and Luke mutters something under his breath causing Amber to smack his chest. I take Dawn's hand and tug her onto my hospital bed. A sharp pain shoots through my injured shoulder as I adjust to allow her room, ignoring the pain. I need to hold her.

"I don't know what to say," I confess wrapping my good arm around her and tucking her into my chest. "I'm excited."

"Me too," she whispers her bewitching blue eyes full of happiness peer up at me. No longer is there fear or sadness, just pure bliss.

"Marry me?"

"You can't propose like that you jackwagon." Burns cries raising his hands in an uproar. "Get your lazy ass out of bed and get down on one knee."

"Do not get out of bed," Amber warns shooting Burns a scathing glare. "How about we let them have a moment alone."

"I want to know what she's going to say." Burns protests throwing Amber an equally intimidating stare.

"Yes. I say yes," Dawn laughs, and I can't help but join in. Everyone crowds in around us saying their congratulations but all I can think about is how complete my life is becoming. I'm going to be a father. Dawn is mine and will soon be mine forever.

"Marry me tomorrow," I blurt out because I can't wait for a wedding. I need to make her mine right now. She has become so vital to me and now she is carrying my child. I need to make this happen and now.

"How about we focus on getting you better, then we can talk about a wedding," Dawn recommends, wrapping her arm around my waist and squeezing.

"You should get married at Benny's. It's where it all began." Burns offers while ladling more chowder. "Miss Janet can make your cake."

"No, she will get married somewhere nice," Sarah throws out and everyone bursts out with suggestions. Even Eric offers his two cents. I ignore them all and look deep into Dawn's bewitching blue eyes and picture our forever.

Acknowledgements

Deepest love and appreciation to my family who has supported me while I venture down this amazing journey. I love you all so much.

Madelyn you have been a great sounding board, thank you. You are an amazing woman and I am so very proud of you.

To my husband thank you for your support and encouragement.

Rachael Leissner you came to me in my hour of need and have been a tremendous help! Thank you so much! I appreciate everything you have done and feel so lucky we were able to connect.

The Next Step PR, thank you for promoting my book and providing some much-needed guidance. You ladies are amazing, and I am so happy I was able to work with you all.

To my readers, thank you for taking the time to read and share my book. I am so grateful to each and every one of you!

About The Author

Amanda Lee Dixon lives in the weather crazed Midwest with her husband, three teenagers and two mouthy malamutes. When she isn't working on the Peak Valley Forever Series, she is obsessively reading romance and fantasy books or pen shopping. Her weaknesses are colorful pens, planners and coffee.

Connect with Amanda now:
Website: www.amandaleedixon.com

Protect Forever